BAD BLOOD

By the same author

The Wrath of Kane

BAD BLOOD

G.T. DUNN

ROBERT HALE · LONDON

© G.T. Dunn 1995
First published in Great Britain 1995

ISBN 0 7090 5546 3

Robert Hale Limited
Clerkenwell House
Clerkenwell Green
London EC1R 0HT

The right of G.T. Dunn to be identified as
author of this work has been asserted by him
in accordance with the Copyright, Designs and
Patents Act 1988.

Photoset in North Wales by
Derek Doyle & Associates, Mold, Clwyd.
Printed and bound in Great Britain by
WBC Book Manufacturers Limited,
Bridgend, Mid-Glamorgan.

BAD BLOOD

ONE

From out of a blue, cloudless sky the burning hot sun beat down unmercifully onto the backs of the small column of soldiers. There was not even the merest hint of a cooling breeze present to ease the suffering of the tired, sweat-sodden troopers as they continued to escort the covered buckboard across the seemingly endless expanse of dry, dusty plain.

In the distance a lone buzzard circled on a rising current of air and surveyed the apparently barren land below. As it floated along effortlessly high above the ground it suddenly spotted a careless young prairie dog that had strayed too far from the protection of the main colony. In an instant the bird dived earthward towards its unsuspecting, defenceless target. All too late the adults in the group cried out a warning.

Before the youngster had time to react it was plucked from the ground in the sharp talons of the bird and carried high up into the air. It gave a helpless, pitiful squeal as it tried, unsuccessfully, to struggle against the crushing grip of the talons. As the bird winged its way south away from the patrol it noticed a rocky outcrop just to the east of its flight path. It carried its prize to the craggy escarpment. On arrival it released its catch and watched as it fell and dashed itself against the rocks far below. The buzzard then landed beside the dead prairie dog and ate its fill in unhurried fashion before returning to patrol the skies.

Apart from the buzzard and the vehicle with its six-man escort, nothing else stirred on the scorched land. The other prairie dogs had wisely retreated to their burrows. All the other critters indigenous to the plains of northern Texas were holed up in shady retreats waiting for the cool of evening.

The troopers had spent the best part of two weary, bone-jarring, rump-sore days in the saddle. Their blue tunics were caked in sweat and trail-dust. To a man their throats felt parched and their minds numbed by the boredom of the ride. Nothing untoward had happened since they had left Fort Walsh on their routine mission to escort the lieutenant to the stage depot at Miller Springs.

It didn't fit the glamorous image of life in the U.S. Cavalry, but in reality it was what such a career was all about. Long, repetitive periods of monotony and boredom followed by short, violent interludes was the way of things for 'A' troop, 5th United States Cavalry, just as it was for all the other units scattered across the west to protect the growing tide of migrants and settlers.

Most of the troopers were lost in their own thoughts when the lieutenant called a halt. As soon as he heard the officer's shouted order to take a brief water-break, Sergeant Hobbs reined in his mount. As the rest of the troop came to a halt the sergeant waved his hand as a signal for them to dismount and relax. He then rode back to where the lieutenant was slowly climbing out of the rig to stretch his cramped limbs.

'How much further to Miller Springs?' he asked as the sergeant pulled his mount up alongside him.

'I'd say not much more than a couple of hours, Lieutenant Ratcliffe,' replied Hobbs as he eased himself down out of the saddle.

'Then I should be in good time for the four o'clock stage,' observed Ratcliffe contentedly, as he beat the dust from his pants with his white, army issue gauntlets.

'No doubt about it, sir,' agreed Hobbs as he reached deep into the right-hand pocket of his britches for the makings of a smoke. Ratcliffe declined his offer of tobacco and paper. Instead he reached back into the buckboard for his canteen. He took a long swig of the stale, warm water while Hobbs nimbly rolled a cigarette in his short, thick fingers.

'Beats me why anyone would want to live in this country,' remarked Ratcliffe as he surveyed the vast stillness before his eyes. The grass and sagebrush were sandy-coloured from months without rain. Apart from a rocky outcrop some miles distant and a few scattered cottonwood trees, the land was totally flat and characterless in all directions.

'The Comanches like it,' advised Hobbs as he struck a match to light his cigarette.

'They can have it,' offered Ratcliffe without a second thought. He took another drink from his canteen and then used his forearm to wipe the screen of sweat from his sunburnt brow. The lieutenant didn't really like the sergeant. He had never been able to come to terms with his brusque manner and general lack of respect for authority. But there was no denying that he was a good soldier when the chips were down.

He climbed aboard the buckboard and settled himself down on the hard, wooden bench-seat facing forward. At least he had the shade of the canvas top to protect him from the worst extremes of the heat and dust.

He was lost in his own thoughts as the little group resumed their journey to Miller Springs. His mind focused on the girl back home in Missouri. The one he was going to see for the first time in eighteen months. He instinctively reached for the gold pocket-watch which he always kept inside his tunic. As he flipped the timepiece open he gazed longingly at the happy, smiling face of his girl. A fading picture and an irregular exchange of letters were no substitute for having her beside him, but time and distance had not cooled the flame of love that burned within his heart. He hoped that she would feel the same way when they were reunited.

It was a little after two-thirty in the afternoon when Miller Springs came into view. Every time Ratcliffe visited the bustling settlement it seemed to have sprouted another dwelling or place of business. They had even got around to adding a proper wooden sidewalk.

Before the war it had been home to fewer than fifty people, but in the years since it had become a thriving commercial centre. The recent additions of a church and a schoolhouse provided it with a necessary touch of refinement. The inhabitants claimed it gave them a genuine air of civilization. It was merely a façade though, for the goings-on in the two rival saloons on Main Street were usually anything but civilized.

The column rode into town a full hour and a half before the eastbound stage was due to leave. Main Street was full of ordinary people going about their daily business. A few anxious glances were cast in their direction, for all too often in the past a visit from the bluecoats of Fort Walsh had led to trouble. Off-duty soldiers had a reputation for hard drinking and womanizing. Such conduct inevitably led to conflict with the locals.

One of those who wore a worried frown was the town sheriff, Pat Blaine. He was a hard-nosed, tough, no-quarter-asked no-quarter-given sort of lawman. Within the community he was respected rather than liked. There were many who considered him arrogant and a touch too ruthless. But they couldn't argue that he kept order.

He wasn't the fastest man with a gun, but he was quick enough. What he lacked in speed he more than made up for in intelligence, cunning and downright meanness.

Those who lived outside the law knew of, and feared, his reputation. Even the tough, brawling frontier-soldiers from Fort Walsh didn't relish the prospect of taking on the wide-shouldered, six-foot-two-inch, two-hundred-and-thirty-pound lawman with fists of steel and a temper to match. At least not until they had sunk enough cold beers and hard liquor to provide them with the necessary Dutch courage.

The lawman stood motionless on the sidewalk outside his office, leaning against an upright wooden post as the soldiers rode on past him. He recognized the burly shape of the sergeant at the head of the troop. They had had several run-ins in the past. The soldier still carried a scar just above his left ear, courtesy of Blaine.

Blaine waited until the troopers reached the stage depot before he made his move. 'Bob,' he called loudly.

'Yeah,' came the reply. His young deputy, Bob Bates, appeared in the doorway of the office. 'What d'ya need?'

'Nothing,' replied Blaine. 'Just mind the store for a while. I've got some business to take care of.'

'You dragged me all the way out here just to tell me to mind the office. Why didn't ya just holler?'

Blaine gave a rueful grin. 'You spend too much time sitting in your damn chair and not enough time doing what I pay you to do. Figured I'd just make sure you weren't asleep!'

The deputy gave a mocking laugh. He caught sight of the soldiers down at the depot. 'What are they doing in town?' he asked, spitting out into the dry street.

'That's just what I aim to find out,' replied Blaine, moving towards the depot.

'You want me to go with you?'

'No. What I want is for you to do what I told you. Stay put. I'll be back presently.'

Ratcliffe was inside the depot when Blaine approached his men. Having paid for his ticket he stepped outside to see what all the fuss was about. Everyone fell silent when he appeared in the doorway. 'Is there a problem, sheriff?' he asked, from the top step.

'Nope,' replied Blaine casually. 'Just making

sure you soldier-boys don't create one.'

Ratcliffe didn't like the man's attitude. But he had to concede the lawman had just cause to be somewhat officious; after all, the soldiers of Fort Walsh had not exactly endeared themselves to the townsfolk with their conduct in recent months. The lieutenant nodded. 'I'm due out on the next stage. My men will leave town within the hour,' he advised Blaine, meeting the lawman's stare head-on.

'But lieutenant!' exclaimed Hobbs. 'The men are hot and tired, not to mention dry. A few beers and a good night's sleep wouldn't go amiss before we set off back to the fort.'

'You heard me, sergeant,' snapped Ratcliffe. 'You've my permission to have a couple of beers right now to wash the dust from your throats. But the very second the stage leaves town you saddle up and ride. Is that clearly understood?'

Hobbs nodded, but he didn't look at all happy. 'Yes sir,' he replied. The troopers immediately made off in the direction of the Lucky Lady.

'I'm obliged,' said Blaine, pushing his hat further back on his head.

'Some elements of the 5th might have earned us a dubious reputation, but most of the men are decent and law-abiding.'

'I'll take your word for it,' replied Blaine.

Ratcliffe shook his head. He brushed past Blaine and made his way off to the town's other saloon. Ratcliffe found the Last Chance Saloon almost deserted. After ordering a beer he settled himself at a table in the far corner of the room. The beer wasn't particularly cold, but it was better than the stale water he had endured on the trail. When his glass was empty he returned it to the counter and left to check on his men.

Outside in the street he became aware of a sudden change in the weather. Although it was still very humid, the wind had got up from the north. Dark, billowing clouds were massing on the horizon. A storm was blowing in. He knew it would hit about the time the soldiers were due to return to the fort. Forked lightning and flash floods were obstacles they could do without. The situation called for a quiet word in the sheriff's ear.

He found Blaine in his office with his feet up on the desk, chawing on the end of a half-smoked cigar. The lawman never budged an inch when he walked in. 'Bad storm brewing,' Ratcliffe announced very matter-of-factly.

'So what?' retorted an uninterested Blaine.

Ratcliffe removed his white cavalry hat and began to twirl it about his fingers. 'Look, Blaine, I know you don't much care for the army, but as long as me and my men cause you no trouble I don't see why you can't be a little more reasonable.'

'You saying I ain't being reasonable?' responded Blaine. He swung his feet down from the desk and stood up. His fierce brown eyes narrowed as he waited for a response.

'Let's just say you haven't been exactly over-friendly.'

'I might have been if you hadn't had that fat sergeant with you.'

'Hobbs?'

'Yeah.'

'You know him?'

'Yeah. I've had several run-ins with him in the past. Strikes me as a real bad-ass.'

'Can't say I'm fond of him myself,' admitted Ratcliffe. 'He's been busted back to private twice to my knowledge. But he's army through and through. Knows the territory, knows how to handle men, and he sure as hell knows a thing or two when it comes to fighting Comanches. I don't think he'll give you any trouble this trip.'

'I know he won't. He's leaving town when you do!'

'Blaine, you know as well as I do what a norther's like after a dry spell. The storm will hit right about the time they make it across the Little Snake River. Let them wait it out here until morning.'

'Nothing doing.'

Ratcliffe scratched his chin. He met Blaine's determined stare. It was obvious he wasn't about to give in unless the lieutenant came up with some sure-fire way of guaranteeing his wayward sergeant's behaviour. 'What if they stay out of the saloons and just hole up some place warm and dry until the storm passes by?'

'How you gonna guarantee they'll do that?' demanded Blaine.

'I'll give them a direct order.'

Blaine laughed. 'You think they'll obey it once you're gone?'

'They're army, they'll obey.'

Blaine turned away and strolled to the far end of his office. 'All right,' he said. 'As long as they stay put in Jake Slocombe's livery stable they can wait it out. But they leave the moment the storm clears.' Ratcliffe nodded in agreement. He promptly left without another word to break the news to his men.

When he entered the Lucky Lady he found five of his troopers ensconced at a corner table talking quietly amongst themselves and Hobbs in the arms of Big Sal, the resident whore. To a man the troopers stood up as their officer approached the table. 'Sergeant! A word in your ear, if you will!' he barked, as he halted by the table.

'Can't it wait?' growled Hobbs as he continued to try and give Sally his undivided attention.

'No it can't,' snapped Ratcliffe.

Hobbs turned to face him. For a moment it seemed he was going to say something, but then he thought better of it. He pushed himself away from Sal and slouched over to the table. 'My apologies, sir. I didn't mean no disrespect.'

Instantly the lieutenant recoiled from the smell of alcohol on the man's breath. It confirmed what he had suspected, that the sergeant was well-oiled. Without liquor Hobbs was a difficult, often truculent non-commissioned officer, but still a darned good one. But with a few drinks inside him he became aggressive, surly and potentially very dangerous. On the post the strict routine and discipline of army life kept him at arm's length from his nemesis. Once in town, however, the task of keeping him dry became that much more difficult.

'You reek of whiskey,' advised Ratcliffe in disgust. 'I thought I told you to keep it to a beer or two?'

'Beer's no fit drink for a sergeant of the United States Cavalry,' stated Hobbs.

'If Blaine sees you in this state he'll slap you in

jail so quick your feet will hardly touch the ground.'

'I'd like to see him try it.'

'From what he tells me he's already done it a time or two.'

'This time I'll be ready for him.'

'No you won't. I don't want any trouble. Any fighting or public disturbance of any kind and I'll have you busted all the way back to private. This time for good. And with time in the stockade thrown in just for good measure. Got the message, sergeant?'

A sarcastic grin that bordered on insolence formed on the man's face. 'Yes sir,' he replied with a slow, measured salute.

'I'm giving all you men a direct order. There's a storm brewing. The sheriff has agreed to let you remain in town until it blows over. You will go with me now to the livery stable down the street. There you will remain until the storm passes. Then you will mount up and ride directly back to the fort. Is that clearly understood?'

'Yes sir,' chorused the troopers in unison.

'Right then, let's get you settled in the livery stable.' With that Ratcliffe led them away at a brisk pace. At the door Hobbs turned and blew a kiss to Big Sal. She didn't need any telling that he intended returning when the coast was clear.

Blaine was present when the eastbound stage pulled out at four. Before the dust had even settled in the street he strolled away in search of the soldiers. The lawman entered the livery stable through the judas gate in the main door. He found the soldiers lying around on some straw bales. Two of them had hats pulled down over their eyes and were clearly asleep. The rest were talking amongst themselves. They fell quiet when they caught sight of him.

'Can we help you?' asked Hobbs, rising up from the ground to stand defiantly at the head of the soldiers. He spat out his chewing-tobacco. It landed with an undignified splat inches from the lawman's right boot. Blaine ignored the provocation. He did, however, draw attention to the Winchester he cradled lovingly in his arms.

'Just making sure you boys were comfortable,' he replied with a bland expression.

'What more could a man want?' sneered Hobbs.

'I know what you want, sergeant, but you ain't getting it this trip,' warned Blaine. He was giving Hobbs his undivided attention. Despite Ratcliffe's assurance he wasn't convinced the sergeant would obey orders.

'Now see here, sheriff, we're under orders as you well know.' The way he said it left Blaine in absolutely no doubt that Hobbs was set on causing trouble.

'Just make sure you stay that way,' he advised. 'I've already put one crease in your thick skull, I'd hate to have to give you a matching set.'

Hobbs reflectively touched the scar above his ear and nodded. He hadn't forgotten who had put the dent in his head. It was a matter that troubled him constantly. He had sworn an oath to himself the day it happened that he'd pay the sheriff back with interest.

'Remember, stay put until the storm ends and then get the hell out of here,' said Blaine. With that he backed away slowly, never once turning his back on Hobbs until he was out in the street.

'Better take it easy, sarge,' advised Private Gannon from the comfort of a straw bale. 'The sheriff doesn't seem to be the kind of man we should tangle with.'

'Shut your mouth,' snapped Hobbs.

'Hey,' interceded the veteran Trooper York, 'both of you cool it. We have our orders, Hobbs. Let's just sit it out and do like we was told.'

'Who asked you, old man?' demanded Hobbs in a fit of pique. 'If you think I'm gonna stay cooped up in here when I could be having a right good time with my gal Sally you must be off your head.'

'Ratcliffe will have you broken if you go within a hundred yards of the Lucky Lady,' warned York. The others murmured in agreement.

'What Ratcliffe don't know about won't hurt him,' said Hobbs. 'I'm gonna pay my Sal a visit just as soon as we've had something to eat. Who's with me?'

At first his question met with empty stares. Finally, after what seemed like an eternity, young Daniel Baker spoke in support of the sergeant's stand. 'Hell, I'm with you. Anything's better than staying in this rat-trap.'

'Don't be stupid, kid,' scolded York. 'You're heading for trouble. Hell, Hobbs, you know that lawman is just waiting for you to pull a fool stunt like that.'

'Since when has a cavalryman been pushed about by a damned lawman?' asked Phil Cooper, rising from the floor to stand beside Hobbs and Baker. 'I'm with you, sarge.'

'Anyone else fancy having some fun?' pressed Hobbs with a huge grin.

'I've got a bad feeling about this, Hobbs. I

reckon you'd best reconsider,' advised York.

'Screw you, old man. We're going. You can suit yourself.'

That effectively ended the debate. The troopers were split right down the middle. Hobbs, Cooper and Baker were set on returning to the Lucky Lady while the old campaigner York and his two buddies, the Irishman Pat Gannon and the ex-rebel Johnny Halliday, were equally determined to follow orders and stay out of trouble.

By the time they broke open their cold rations a few minutes later, the storm was beginning to unleash its full, pent-up fury on the town.

TWO

First came the thunder, then streaks of forked lightning and finally the rain. The storm quickly turned day into night. It rained so hard that it was almost impossible to see from one side of the street to the other. Huge raindrops bounced back off the hard, dusty streets to a height of several inches. The sound was as deafening as a herd of stampeding cattle. Soon a river, several inches deep, was flowing through the centre of town.

From within the sanctuary of the livery stable Hobbs and the other troopers surveyed the scene through a hole in the wall. A clap of thunder exploded almost directly overhead. Almost immediately a streak of lightning briefly illuminated the darkened street. 'Sweet Jesus,' yelled Baker above the noise of the storm.

'Been a while since I've seen a storm to match this one,' said Gannon as he retreated from the doorway.

'Hell, this ain't nothing like the ones we used to get back in Missouri,' advised Cooper.

'You surely ain't going out in this?' asked York, hoping that the storm's timely intervention would dissuade Hobbs from his chosen course.

'Nothing's gonna keep me from my Sal,' replied

Hobbs with a grin. 'Definitely not a little drop of rain.'

They continued watching the rain become ever harder, the thunder ever louder and the lightning ever more frequent and brighter. After ten minutes Hobbs became impatient. 'Can't wait any longer,' he announced to the others, as he pulled on his slicker. 'Sal's a-waiting on me.'

Cooper immediately followed suit. Baker hesitated, took another lingering look at the weather and then joined them. York moved across to intercept the burly sergeant. He placed a hand on his shoulder and looked him directly in the eye. 'Are you sure you want to do this?' he asked.

Hobbs stood his ground. He roughly removed York's hand from his shoulder and said, 'Don't ever lay a hand on me again, old man, or I'll break it in two.' With that he pushed past, opened the judas gate and stepped out into the rain. 'You coming?' he called back over his shoulder to Cooper and Baker. The two troopers looked at each other and then at the sergeant. They nodded and followed.

'You're a couple of fools,' yelled York angrily, as they strolled away.

The three soldiers had to hold their hands up to protect their faces from the stinging, driving rain. By the time they made it to the saloon their slickers, pants and boots were thoroughly soaked.

The Lucky Lady was playing host to a dozen or more people trapped by the storm. Ned Bennett was not exactly surprised to see Hobbs reappear. He knew the sergeant well enough to suspect he would disobey his officer. Before the troopers had even taken off their slickers and hats the proprietor had poured out a couple of beers and a whiskey. 'I'd just about given up on you boys,' said a smiling Bennett as the troopers approached the counter.

'You ain't short of custom tonight,' remarked Hobbs, downing the whiskey in one swallow. His sharp eyes quickly scanned the room. No one seemed to be paying the soldiers any heed. 'Blaine been in?'

Bennett continued smiling. 'No. He doesn't like getting his feet wet unless he has to.'

Hobbs nodded and then jabbed a finger at his empty tumbler. 'Fill it up,' he said, reaching deep into his britches pocket. 'And give my friends another beer as soon as they're ready.'

'Sure the kid shouldn't be on sarsaparilla?' joked the bartender.

Baker's innocent blue eyes immediately registered anger. He made a move towards Bennett, intent on exacting an apology for the insult.

'Take it easy, kid, Ned's only funning,' said Hobbs, putting out a restraining arm. The boy scowled. His hurt pride meant it was not until some three beers later that he forgot the insult.

Hobbs knocked back half the contents of his second drink. He set the tumbler back on the bar and had another look about the room. 'Where's Sal?' he demanded.

'Where else but upstairs waiting for you,' advised Bennett with a broad grin that displayed all his yellow, rotting teeth.

Hobbs nodded in satisfaction. 'Give me a bottle and a couple of glasses,' he said. Bennett obliged him and then waved cheerfully as he disappeared up the wooden staircase to the rooms above. A moment later Hobbs disappeared from sight into the bedroom on the left to raucous cheers from his two friends below.

'Well it's about time,' said a scantily dressed Sally from her reclined position on the bed.

'All good things come to those who wait,' he replied. He placed the bottle of whiskey and the glasses on the side-table and started to unbutton his tunic.

Sally rose from the bed and glided across the room towards him. In an instant she had her hands on the buckle of his leather belt. Having removed his jacket and shirt he sat down on the bed while she first pulled off his sodden boots and then his damp trousers. Within seconds they were huddled up together under the sheets making love noisily.

'How was it?' she asked after they had disentangled their limbs and were lying breathless and motionless at each other's side.

'As good as always, Sal,' he replied without a second thought. Then, after a momentary pause, he added, 'You're the best girl, you always have been.'

She giggled and snuggled back into him. 'You want to go again?' she asked, kissing him lightly on the cheek.

'Later,' he replied. 'You've plumb tuckered me out for now.'

Sally giggled again like a little girl. Hobbs reached for the bottle and poured two equal measures. He handed one to Sal and knocked back his own in one swallow. As the whore sipped on her whiskey he refilled his glass. He toyed with it for a moment and then set it down on the table.

'Maybe we should make love again before I become too drunk to enjoy it,' he said, rolling over to face her. She simply and willingly complied.

Blaine was impatient for the storm to end. It wasn't that he objected to all the rain, heck no one in the territory could argue that it wasn't sorely needed, but what he did mind was the presence of the soldiers. The fact was, he didn't trust the sergeant. He had an uneasy feeling about things and wasn't about to relax until he saw the back of him.

Around six he decided to check out the two saloons. Given that the storm was still raging overhead it was the last thing he would normally have done, but his sense of unease had persisted and he therefore felt obliged to make sure all was well.

'Where the hell are you going?' asked Bates, on seeing his boss reach for his hat and slicker.

'For a walk,' came the reply.

'In this weather?'

'Think it's about time I checked out the Lucky Lady.'

'Well if you've a mind to catch your death of cold I might as well join you.' Bates was halfway out of his chair by the stove when Blaine waved him away.

'No. Stay put. No sense in us both getting wet. Besides, if trouble brews elsewhere in town someone's got to man the office so we get to hear of it.' Bates shrugged his shoulders and sat back down. Blaine took his Winchester from the rack on the wall and, after checking it was loaded, put it beneath his slicker to keep it dry.

There was no sign of a let-up in the rain as

Blaine stepped out onto the sidewalk. The thunder wasn't as loud, nor the lightning so bright or close. A good-sized stream flowed through the very middle of the street. On either side of the main torrent hundreds of large-sized puddles were dotted about for the length and breadth of the entire thoroughfare. Blaine's brown slicker failed to prevent some of the water from soaking the lower reaches of his pants as he hurriedly made his way along the uncovered sidewalk towards the Lucky Lady.

Cooper and Baker were drinking at the bar with their backs to the door when Blaine entered. The enraged lawman spotted them straight away. He strode purposefully towards them with only one thought in mind. Bennett was serving a customer at the far end of the counter, so he had no opportunity to warn the soldiers.

Cooper casually turned his head to survey the room just before Blaine reached him. 'Oh shit!' he exclaimed. He unwisely reached for the flap covering his pistol. Before his hand made contact with his weapon Blaine swung the long barrel of his Winchester in a vicious upward arc to smash into the side of his face. Cooper went spinning to the ground. He lay on the floor groaning loudly as blood poured from a gaping gash in his cheek.

Baker instinctively backed up a couple of steps. The only sound in the room was the ticking of the clock on the wall above the bar. 'I ain't done nothing wrong,' he said, throwing up his hands to show that he wasn't intent on making any trouble.

'What are you doing in here, boy?' demanded Blaine, pointing the Winchester at his chest.

'I just came in for a couple of drinks. I didn't

mean any harm, honest.'

'You were told to stay put in the livery stable.'

'I'm sorry, I truly am. I'll go quietly, I don't want any trouble.'

'You should have thought of that before you came in here.'

'You can't kill me for having a drink?' screamed Baker. He was deathly afraid. It showed in his face and his shaking body. All he could think of was Blaine's reputation for dealing ruthlessly with those who crossed his path.

The sudden creaking of a loose floorboard caused Blaine to shift his gaze upwards to the landing directly ahead of him. His eyes narrowed as they fell upon the familiar shape above him. 'You,' he said. 'You're the cause of all this.'

'Guess I am,' replied Hobbs. The sergeant was dressed in just his moth-eaten long johns. He stood stock-still with his arms resting against the carved oak bannister that ran the length of the landing. It was the sight of the Army Colt filling the soldier's right hand that caused the lawman to hesitate momentarily.

'You're drunk,' shouted Blaine.

'Don't you believe it,' replied Hobbs. An evil grin appeared on his face. 'Make any sort of a move and I'll prove I'm sober by drilling you where you stand.'

Blaine ignored the painful moan emanating from the stricken private at his feet and kept his attention squarely on the sergeant. 'Throw down the pistol, Hobbs, and save yourself a parcel of grief,' he advised, slowly adjusting the position of the Winchester that he cradled in his hands.

'Not on your life,' said Hobbs. 'I figure I'm

dealing the cards in this game. So you'll do as I say. And the first thing I want you to do is to lower the barrel of that gun you're so fond of before I blow it out of your hands.'

The lawman was brave, but he wasn't stupid. He knew that Hobbs had the drop on him. Had he tried to take him out, the sergeant's Colt would have got him before he could bring the rifle to bear. Blaine allowed the Winchester to slowly rotate downwards so that the barrel pointed directly at the floor. 'What now?' he asked, staring into the big soldier's cold, expressionless eyes.

'Drop the rifle and come up here and join me,' instructed Hobbs. Before he could obey one of the cowpokes standing by a table in the centre of the room decided to intervene. Baker was the first to see the gun coming clear of its holster.

'Look out, sarge!' he screamed, reaching for his own pistol. Hobbs reacted with the speed of a striking rattler. With the deftest of movements he brought his own gun to bear on the young cowpoke just as his pistol cleared leather. The whole room seemed to explode as the Army Colt spat fire and lead. Hobbs' single shot hit the cowboy in the middle of the chest, sending him spinning lifelessly away, backwards over the table.

'You son-of-a-bitch,' yelled Blaine. Instantly, in one swift movement, he brought the Winchester up to his waist and fired at the sergeant. But Hobbs was too quick for him. As Blaine fired, Hobbs threw himself to the floor, rolled over once and came up on one knee with his pistol cocked and ready. His unexpectedly sharp reflexes and speed of movement caused the sheriff to shoot high and wide. He never got a second chance. From his kneeling position high above the floor, Hobbs took careful aim and shot Blaine in the belly.

'Nobody move,' warned the sergeant as he came erect.

'For God's sake, somebody help me, I'm gut-shot!' screamed Blaine. He squirmed about in agony on the bloodstained floor. Off to his left Cooper was regaining his senses. He climbed rather unsteadily to his feet and momentarily leaned in ungainly fashion against the bar. It took a few minutes for his head to stop swimming. He wiped the blood from his cheek and spat out a broken tooth. When the mist finally cleared from his eyes he stared about him in a state of confusion.

'You okay?' asked Baker.

'What the hell happened?' demanded the head-sore trooper.

'He hit you,' replied the young soldier, pointing at the moaning, writhing body on the ground before them.

'You ugly bastard,' snarled Cooper. He stepped forward and kicked the lawman in the head. Blaine cried out loudly and then lapsed into unconsciousness.

'If you're through having your fun I suggest it's time we were leaving,' remarked an amused Hobbs, as he started to descend the staircase, keeping a wary eye and a levelled gun on the other customers in the room.

Big Sal appeared at the top of the stairs at the very moment her boyfriend made it to the bar. 'Here,' called Sal, 'you might need these.' She threw the big man's clothes down after him.

'I hope there's still some money left in my pockets,' he said with a grin.

'It's all there, you big ox,' she replied, pretending to be offended by his remark.

After hurriedly dressing himself he reached into his pocket and took out a ten-dollar bill. 'This is for you, darling. I'll leave it right here on the bar,' he said, placing the damp note under an empty glass. She gave a grand bow in appreciation and blew him a kiss. 'Now boys,' he said, addressing himself to the assembled throng of cowboys and businessmen, 'we'll be taking our leave of you. If you value your skins I'd advise against sticking your heads out of the door in the next ten minutes. Anyone does anything foolish and you can be sure you won't live long enough to tell your grandchildren about it.'

Having collected their slickers they took it in turns to dress while keeping the room covered. Hobbs then ordered everyone present to lay their guns on the table in the middle of the room. Next he made them move away to the far end of the bar. When the locals were all at a safe distance the soldiers collected up all the guns and slowly backed away towards the door. 'Don't forget, stay put for ten minutes and no one need get hurt,' said Hobbs. With that he stepped through the door and joined his companions.

The doors continued to swing to and fro, aided by the wind, long after the soldiers had taken their leave. No one inside the Lucky Lady attempted to follow the troopers. They all gathered about the still body of the sheriff and discussed what to do next.

'We got to get the doc for Pat. He's in a bad way,'

said Pete Reynolds, one of the cowhands who had taken shelter in the saloon to wait out the storm.

'You go get Doc Kline if you've a mind to. But I for one ain't setting foot outside that door for a good while yet,' said Bennett. The others either nodded or murmured in agreement. The sergeant's bluff had bought him and his friends some valuable time.

The soldiers stepped out into the howling wind and driving rain. They threw the guns they had confiscated from the saloon out into the muddy street. Hobbs was fairly certain his warning would prevent any of the men inside the Lucky Lady from leaving until the soldiers were well clear of the place. However, he didn't allow his companions to dawdle as they moved off down the sidewalk.

They made it safely to the livery stable without further incident. Hobbs stood directly in front of the door to prevent Cooper and Baker from entering. 'The others are going to want to know what happened,' said Hobbs, after a brief pause to catch his breath. 'Leave all the talking to me. We got to be saddled and out of here within minutes or we'll be dead men.'

'What are we gonna do?' pleaded Baker. For a moment his companions thought he was going to break down in tears. The boy was only eighteen years old and as green as they came. Six months in the army had done little to change that. He was also very easily led, which is why he had followed Hobbs to the Lucky Lady.

'What we are going to do, boy, is get the drop on our friends inside and get the hell out of here just as fast as we can,' replied the sergeant assertively.

'Then what?' asked Cooper.

'Mexico,' stated Hobbs with a grin. 'The land of tequila and pretty senoritas. Then, when things get quietened down, maybe we'll head for the goldfields and do a little prospecting.'

'But that'll make us deserters. The army'll shoot us for sure,' said Baker in alarm.

'Hell, kid, we got no choice. According to the law we're all murderers. We have to make a run for it before we get our necks stretched,' replied Hobbs.

'I ain't killed no one!' exclaimed Baker.

'That ain't how the law will see it,' said Cooper. 'You got to see sense, kid. We're in this together. Hell, I don't know about you but this man's army has suddenly lost its appeal.'

'Cooper's right. Now quit stalling or we'll leave you behind to face the townsfolk on your own,' warned Hobbs.

Baker wiped the rain away from his face where it had run down over the brim of his drooping hat. 'All right,' he agreed. The sergeant checked his gun and then entered the livery stable through the judas gate.

The interior of the building smelt dank and musty. York, Gannon and Halliday were seated on bales of straw playing cards by the light of the single oil-lamp. None of the card-players made any move to acknowledge the arrival of the newcomers. But the distinctive sound of a pistol hammer being cocked instantly drew their full attention.

'What is this?' demanded York, throwing his cards down in front of him.

'Throw your guns on the floor,' said Hobbs.

'What the hell's got into you, Hobbs?' asked

Gannon, rising up from his seat.

'Just stay sitting and do as you're told,' replied Hobbs.

'Do as he says,' advised York. He knew something was up.

Cooper collected their guns. He carried them back to Hobbs. 'Take the cartridges out and then put the guns down by the front door,' Hobbs told him. Cooper obeyed without question, pocketing the slugs he had emptied from the pistols. 'Help Baker saddle our mounts.'

'You going to tell us what this is all about?' asked York.

'Stick around here a while longer and I'm sure you'll find out,' replied Hobbs. 'Get a move on with those damn horses. We need to be moving.'

'All ready,' called Cooper. The three horses were brought forward. Baker pushed open the front door and then mounted. Pulling his hat right down over his face to protect it from the worst of the elements he rode slowly out into the street.

'All clear,' he called back over his shoulder. He wheeled about and stood his horse just outside the door where he could cover York, Gannon and Halliday while his two friends mounted up.

'Be seeing you, boys,' said Hobbs as he eased his mount out through the door.

'I hope you rot in hell, Hobbs,' shouted York as the three men rode off into the gathering gloom.

Gannon ran to the door and peered after the vanishing riders. He swung the door closed and picked up their guns. 'What do you think that was all about?' he asked.

'Damned if I know,' replied York with a shake of his head. 'But I'm sure we'll find out soon enough.'

THREE

You could have cut the atmosphere inside the Lucky Lady with a knife. The badly wounded sheriff moaning and writhing on the floor played on their minds and caused great debate. Everyone knew it was imperative they got medical help for Blaine. But no one was willing to take a chance on sticking their head out of the door. They were paralysed by fear.

For what seemed like an eternity they argued back and forth over what to do. They all left it to each other to seize the initiative. The problem was that they all felt naked without their guns.

Five minutes after the soldiers exited the saloon someone finally grasped the nettle and took positive action. Ben Jordan, one of the silent, brooding cowboys, ran out of patience. He voiced the opinion that the soldiers would not hang around too long outside. It was worth taking a chance to go for help. He was promptly invited to put his theory to the test!

Jordan stealthily and silently slipped out through the back door to check on the lie of the land. He ran around the rear of the building and then edged cautiously along the side alley that ran between the saloon and the barber-shop. One quick glance round the corner confirmed the coast was clear. He walked quickly up to the front entrance and let that be known. Two of his friends, Frank Seeber and Tim Forrest, took off to fetch the doc and Bob Bates. Everyone else sat tight.

Bates was idly rocking in his chair by the stove when Forrest burst into the room nearly taking the door off its hinges. 'What in tarnation is up with you, Tim?' asked the deputy, jumping to his feet.

'Blaine's been shot,' replied Forrest, dripping water onto the floorboards.

'What happened?'

Forrest gave him a brief account of events, after which the deputy moved to his desk and removed a bunch of keys from the top drawer. He then crossed the floor swiftly to the gun-rack on the far wall. After unlocking the padlock and chain he took all six Winchesters from the rack and presented them to Forrest. 'Go hand these out to anyone in the saloon who knows how to use one.'

'Then what?'

'Tell the men to meet me in front of the livery stable.'

'Don't try and go in alone,' warned Forrest, moving towards the door. 'That sergeant is meaner than a cornered rattler.'

'Just get the others,' replied Bates in determined fashion. Without further debate Forrest hurried back to the saloon clutching the guns tightly to his chest. The deputy quickly checked his side-arm and rifle. He then donned his slicker and hurried off in the direction of the livery stable.

As he approached it via the slippery, soaked sidewalk, three horsemen galloped away from the building towards him. Instinctively he raised the Winchester to his shoulder and fired at the riders bearing down on him.

His shot was nervous and hurried. It went harmlessly wide of the mark. All three riders brought their horses to a slithering, sliding halt, grabbed for their guns and started to return fire.

Bates dived for cover behind one of the empty flour-barrels outside Kyte's General Store. From there he got off two more shots, neither of which came remotely close to hitting any of the soldiers. The soldiers' aim was equally bad. The only damage they inflicted was to the windows of the store.

Moments later reinforcements arrived from the Lucky Lady. The newcomers scattered to occupy positions on both sides of the street, from where they opened up on the soldiers. Hobbs constantly whirled his horse about in an attempt to make himself as difficult a target to hit as possible. A bullet tore through the top of Cooper's hat, causing him to duck down instinctively.

Lights came on all over town. An upstairs window opened directly alongside the milling soldiers. A young voice cried out asking what all the shooting was about. Hobbs raised his pistol and fired twice at the opening. There followed a crashing sound as a body fell against some item of furniture.

'Let's get out of here,' yelled Hobbs. He turned his mount and galloped off towards the other end of town with his two companions close behind. A few wild shots accompanied them.

Seeber ran over to where Bates was standing on the sidewalk. 'We gonna go after them?' he asked expectantly as others rushed to join them.

'You bet we are,' growled Bates. 'But first we got to get ourselves organized.'

'What about the other soldiers?' asked Forrest.

'That's right, there were more than three of them came to town,' proclaimed another.

'Well where are they then?' demanded Dave Winter, the son of the town's banker.

'Probably still holed up in the livery stable, I'll bet,' suggested Seeber.

'Let's go find out,' said Bates. With that he led the men forward at a brisk pace, all of them totally oblivious to the heavy rain that continued to fall.

By the time they reached the livery stable the group of ordinary cowhands and family men had become a raging, angry mob with the deputy at their head. They were less than a dozen yards from the building when they saw the judas gate swing open. A soldier poked his head out and peered up the street. Without waiting for any instruction Seeber immediately raised his rifle and fired at the figure in the doorway. The bullet just missed the soldier's head. It went through the wooden wall and ricocheted dangerously around the inside of the livery stable. The soldier instantly ducked back inside, slamming the door closed behind him.

'What the hell did you do that for?' demanded Bates, glaring at Seeber angrily as the mob slowed to a stop all around him.

'I thought he was going to shoot,' replied the cowhand.

'You've cost us the element of surprise,' seethed Bates. Without delay he waved the group forward. They halted right outside the main doors. 'Hey, you inside. This is Deputy Sheriff Bates. I want you to come to the door one at a time and throw your guns out nice and easy.'

'Why did you shoot at us?' asked a nervous voice from inside.

'Never mind that, just do as you're told. There are nine guns out here, so we're well prepared for trouble.'

For the best part of a minute the only sound was the drumming of the rain against the ground. Then, just when the crowd's patience was drawing thin, the judas gate swung open and one after another the soldiers stepped out and dropped their guns on the ground.

'Move away from the door,' advised Bates. The mob escorted the soldiers back inside the livery stable out of the rain. The dim glow from the solitary oil-lamp cast a weird, yellow light across their faces.

'What's going on?' asked York nervously.

'You know full well,' replied the deputy.

'None of us has left here since the lieutenant caught the stage, so we've no idea what you're after,' advised York.

'That's your story,' said Bates. 'I say you and your friends gunned down Sheriff Blaine and a young cowboy in the Lucky Lady not more than fifteen minutes ago.'

'You're crazy,' retorted Gannon, stepping forward to confront the brash young lawman. Bates pointed the barrel of his Winchester at him.

'Come any closer and you're a dead man,' he

warned. Gannon backed off a pace and turned to face York.

'This is the sergeant's doing,' he said in disgust.

At that precise moment the group was joined by another of the townsfolk. Tom Harmer, who owned the hardware store, arrived with a double-barrelled shotgun in his hands and a look of pure hate on his face. 'Are these the ones who killed my young nephew?' he demanded, in a voice full of pent-up rage. One look and they could all tell that he was fighting hard to hold back his tears. His eyes were red and had a strange glazed quality to them.

'Your nephew?' queried Bates, looking puzzled.

'That's right. I guess the ruckus out in the street must have woken him up. He opened the window to see what was happening and one of these bastards shot him. The boy was only thirteen years old.'

'I'm real sorry, Tom,' said Bates with a sad shake of his head.

'How the hell am I ever gonna tell his folks what happened? They only sent him west for a few months because our climate seemed ideal to help him get over a bad bout of pneumonia. Now he's dead.'

'They'll pay for it, Tom,' said Seeber. 'You can depend on that.'

'We didn't do it,' pleaded Halliday with fear in his eyes. York swallowed hard. He had seen many examples of frontier justice at first-hand, and he sensed that the soldiers were about to fall foul of it themselves. The deputy's next words only served to confirm his worst fears.

'I reckon they're all to blame. These three and

the ones who got away. We'll take care of these first.'

'What you aiming to do with us?' cried Halliday.

'We're going to hang you,' announced Bates to a loud roar of approval.

'No!' screamed Halliday. He made a desperate run for the side entrance but was caught well short of the door by two of the townsfolk. The rest of the mob swarmed forward to grab hold of York and Gannon to prevent them from taking flight.

'Henry and Joe, go get something to bind their hands. Pete, fetch three good, strong saddle-ropes.'

The men found all they needed for the task within the stable. Soon the soldiers were bound and dragged to a crossbeam in the middle of the building. Nooses were hurriedly, but expertly, tied in the ropes. The ends were then thrown and secured over the beam. Horses were brought forward. The soldiers were unceremoniously bundled into the saddles with the nooses draped around their necks. Harmer took a quirt from one of the other men and made ready to whip the flanks of the horses.

'Any last words?' growled Bates. He spat on the floor and glared at the helpless men.

'You got the wrong men,' stated York in a quaking voice.

'I don't think so,' replied Harmer. His eyes were full of hate.

'How can you do this?' asked York, looking Bates in the eye. 'You're supposed to be a lawman. If you're so sure of our guilt then throw us in jail and let a judge and jury try us in proper fashion.'

'And let some smart army lawyer get you off? No chance.'

Bad Blood

As the soldiers gazed in terror into the eyes of their captors they knew that no amount of reasoning or pleading was going to save them. York sat quietly astride his horse contemplating the vagaries of life. Halliday mumbled something incomprehensible and Gannon closed his eyes.

The mob was so preoccupied with the soldiers they failed to notice the silent arrival of a newcomer. He stood just inside the main entrance, rain dripping steadily from the brim of his hat and jet-black slicker. A brand new Winchester was clasped tightly in his hands. His piercing eyes quickly surveyed the scene.

He was no stranger to trouble and knew exactly how to look after himself when the going got tough. But it was the soldiers, rather than himself, that he was concerned about. He had to find a way of defusing the situation and securing their release. Whatever they had done, he knew they didn't deserve to end their lives in such a fashion, no man did.

'I don't think the army's gonna take kindly to you hanging three of its troopers,' said the newcomer, just loudly enough to gain everyone's full attention.

All heads instantly turned towards him. In different circumstances he would have found the surprised looks to be quite amusing. But it was no time for frivolity. Nobody moved. For a brief moment the silence was almost deafening. Then Bates spoke up clearly and defiantly. 'Who are you? What do you want here?'

'Who I am don't matter. What I want is for you to release those troopers right now.'

'The hell we will, mister. They just killed some

of our people,' growled Seeber.

'If that's the case the army will take care of them.'

'It's our business, not the army's.'

'I don't agree.'

'We don't care whether you agree or not,' said Harmer. 'They killed my nephew and they're gonna pay right here and now.'

'I'm truly sorry about your nephew, but this ain't the way to settle things,' advised the stranger calmly.

'You're butting into things that don't concern you,' warned an increasingly agitated Seeber.

'You are really beginning to piss me off, fella. Start walking a little softer or you might force me to teach you some manners,' retorted the stranger.

'Screw you,' yelled Seeber. He raised his rifle with the plain intention of plugging the meddlesome newcomer. Without hesitation, and seemingly without even aiming, the stranger fired his own gun hitting the irate cowhand in the foot. 'Ouch, oh God, yow!' exclaimed Seeber, as he fell to the floor clutching his right foot. 'The son-of-a-bitch shot my toes off.' He continued to roll around in the muddy straw holding onto his foot with both hands. His friends raised their guns and pointed them at his assailant.

'I wouldn't do anything stupid,' the stranger advised, gently moving the barrel of his gun from side to side to show that he had the whole room covered. 'No doubt you'll kill me if you've a mind to, but I'll take a good few of you with me, starting with the deputy.'

His words caused the mob to freeze. They

looked to Bates for leadership. But for once the arrogant, strong-willed, young lawman's nerve failed him. Pride might have caused him to go for his gun, but that would have been a fatal error of judgement. He knew it, too. 'Who are you?' he asked, motioning to the others to lower their guns.

'I know him,' said Henry Charlery, the tall, round-shouldered owner of the town's small hotel. 'His name's Kane, Sam Kane. He scouts for the army.'

'Another army man!' exclaimed Harmer. 'We should hang him too.'

Sam Kane's face remained expressionless. 'You ain't hanging anyone, friend, I thought I'd already made that plain.'

'Kind of an interesting stand-off we have here,' observed Charlery.

'The question you have to ask yourself is, is this matter worth dying over?' asked Kane, his eyes alert for any sign of trouble.

'What do you suggest we do?' asked one of the other citizens. It was the first clear sign that the group's resolve was beginning to waver.

'Lay down your guns and let me talk this out with the deputy.'

'Might be as well,' agreed Charlery. 'Maybe we are letting our emotions run away with us.'

'Are you prepared to let them get away with it?' demanded Harmer, looking daggers at the hotel-owner.

'No one's gonna get away with anything,' rejoined Kane. 'All I'm asking for is a chance to talk things over with the deputy. Then if these men are truly guilty they'll face the full weight of the law, but in court.'

The men began to talk calmly amongst themselves. Kane's words had taken some of the heat out of the situation. The townsfolk were back under control. They were beginning to see things a little more clearly. Only the silver-haired Harmer seemed unconvinced. But he was a man alone. Without the support of the others he was powerless to act.

'Okay Kane,' said Charlery, 'we're putting our guns up.' One by one the men went and rested their rifles against the nearest wall of the livery stable. Slowly but surely they then began to drift out of the building. Two of them helped the hopping Seeber on his way. At Kane's request Charlery remained behind just long enough to remove the nooses from the troopers' necks and cut the bonds that held their wrists.

When Kane and the deputy were alone with the soldiers the scout went and stood directly in front of the lawman. Bates looked drained and haggard. He didn't like having to look the scout in the eye, for he had lost face in front of his friends and in so doing had learned a great deal about himself. And he didn't much like what he'd found out.

'Want to tell me what happened?' asked Kane.

Bates told him all he knew of the chain of events that had brought him and the townspeople to the livery stable. When he had finished, Kane turned to York and said, 'Is that how you see things?'

The trooper spoke while continuing to massage some life back into his wrists. 'It ain't quite as straightforward as that.' He gave his version of events, leaving nothing out.

'Sounds to me as if you've got the wrong men,' advised Kane, when York had finished speaking.

'Maybe,' agreed Bates somewhat reluctantly. 'But we only have his word for that.'

'Is there any doubt that it was the sergeant who shot the cowboy and the sheriff?'

'None. The witnesses all agree on that point.'

'Then you've got to admit there is every chance this trooper and his friends are telling the truth?'

Bates shrugged his shoulders. He was losing the argument and he knew it. 'Yeah, I guess so.'

'And yet if I hadn't happened along when I did, you would quite happily have hung them.'

The deputy merely nodded and looked down at his boots. 'I ain't proud of my actions. Things just kinda got out of control.'

'It happens,' said Kane. 'But it sure as hell shouldn't.'

'What you aiming to do now?'

'That's partly up to you.'

The lawman shrugged his shoulders. 'Blaine usually makes all the decisions.'

'And I don't suppose he's in any fit state to ask?' queried Kane.

Bates shook his head slowly. 'By all accounts he'll be lucky to see-in the morning.'

Kane nodded, then rubbed his chin thoughtfully. 'I ain't happy about Hobbs and his compadres getting away. No tellin' what desperate men will do. The army also likes to clean house. Can't have deserters left wandering all over the country.'

'I reckon I could round up a posse and go after them.'

'No,' said Kane. 'Me an' these troopers will do that.'

'The townsfolk aren't gonna take kindly to you

riding off with these men. They still hold them at least partly accountable for what happened here.'

'Then you'd better straighten them out pronto,' warned Kane. 'These troopers are riding out with me. I ain't leaving them behind to become sacrificial lambs.'

Bates had no choice but to let the scout have his way. 'Okay, but there's bad blood between the townsfolk and the army. You have to promise to play things straight, Kane.'

'I will,' promised Kane. 'They'll be delivered to Fort Walsh for trial.'

The young lawman had regained some of his self-composure and was therefore growing in confidence. He wasn't entirely satisfied with what the scout had to say. He didn't know him well enough to be sure he could trust him and said as much. They debated the matter back and forth for several minutes before settling on a suitable compromise. Kane agreed to let two of the townsfolk ride with him and the troopers after Hobbs and his friends. The deputy then left and went in search of John Phillips and his friend Hal Brady, two locals whom Blaine occasionally used as extra deputies whenever the need arose. He knew that he would be able to persuade them to ride along with Kane.

'Hobbs is a nasty piece of work, always has been,' observed York as they patiently waited for the deputy to return with his volunteers.

'Can't say that I've spent any time with the man,' replied Kane as he rubbed his calf in an effort to get rid of a sudden bout of cramp brought on by the damp weather and too much time in the saddle.

'Very quick-tempered,' added Halliday. 'Seen him beat a man to a pulp once just for looking at him the wrong way.'

'I think the sergeant's days are numbered,' said Kane.

'We got to catch him first,' advised York.

'We'll catch him,' replied Kane confidently. 'The rain will stop soon and he'll have left us a clear track that a child could follow.'

Bates duly returned some ten minutes later with Phillips and Brady in tow. Kane set out his plan for tracking the fugitives which met with the general approval of all concerned.

'When are you aiming to leave?' asked Phillips when the scout had finished speaking.

'An hour before dawn,' replied Kane.

'Why not now?' queried Brady, who was obviously very keen to take up the chase.

'I'd rather wait for the rain to stop,' replied Kane. 'Besides, it's likely we have a long ride ahead of us, so we might as well get some rest now while we can.'

Brady and Phillips nodded their approval and moved towards the back of the building to find a comfortable spot for the night. Bates left to check on the condition of Sheriff Blaine.

Within the hour everything at Miller Springs fell deathly quiet. It appeared as if the whole population had retired to bed early as a mark of respect for the young nephew of Tom Harmer. One of the few lights that shone out into the night was that of old Doc Kline's. It was there in the back room of his office at a little before midnight that Sheriff Pat Blaine drew his last tortured, pain-racked breath.

FOUR

The Reverend Thomas Fielding felt as if he was carrying the weight of the entire world on his back. Although his immensely tall, broad and powerful frame provided him with a countenance that appeared well up to the task, he was sorely troubled by the responsibility he had recently inherited.

He was truly a stranger in a strange land. For two long, worrying days he had been forced, by circumstances beyond his control, to bear the mantle of command for the mixed band of emigrants out of Catesville, Missouri. He was well-accustomed to the prospect of looking after folks' spiritual needs, but taking charge of a wagon-train was an entirely different kettle of fish.

A dozen prairie schooners of various sizes snaked slowly across the plains loaded down with all the earthly possessions of the families who had put their trust jointly in the Lord and their wagon-master. Thirty-seven God-fearing souls – farmers, storekeepers and former soldiers of the Confederacy – had signed on with the train for the long and perilous journey to the promised land of New Mexico Territory. They all sought the same thing, to carve out a new life for themselves in a virgin land that offered them soil to till and, above everything else, real hope for the future. They left many friends and memories behind them in a community that was still struggling to recover from the ravages of war and the subsequent effects of the northern carpet-baggers who had followed the 'Yankee army of occupation'.

All the way west from Catesville the talk had been of a fresh start, of a new life in a land where their dreams could match the size of the mountains, where things would be different. They would build a new community out of the wilderness. One that would bring security and prosperity to all.

The journey had been fairly easy and uneventful all the way to the Cimarron River. They had experienced nothing more serious than the occasional broken axle or bout of diarrhoea. It was then, as they camped on the banks of the river, that things began to turn sour.

First Jim Berry, their experienced and highly popular trail-guide, disappeared without a trace after going off alone to scout ahead while the weary pilgrims rested up before crossing the mighty river. They sent riders out to try and find him, but no one could find any trace of him. Some of the men reported seeing plenty of Indian sign, so the families concluded that he had fallen into hostile hands.

Had it not been for the calming influence of the reverend a real panic might have set in. But his sonorous voice had rung out around the camp-fire to instil confidence and reason into the assembled crowd.

The very next morning, without warning, cholera struck the wagon-train. Bat Peterson, ex-major in the Army of the Confederacy and the head of the train, was the first to display the telltale symptoms of severe intestinal problems and high fever. He was quickly followed by Emma Grant and her two young children.

It was then, during a hurried, animated conference, that Thomas Fielding, practising minister of the Methodist Church, had command thrust upon him. The role of wagon-master was one he did not covet. But when all was said and done he was as well qualified for the job as any man.

Before the major's fever got a proper hold on him he summoned Fielding and instructed him to keep heading due west with the sun. Such a course, he assured him, would eventually lead them to one of the scattered hamlets on the northern plains, where they would be able to rest up for a while in safety and get medical aid for the sick.

There was plenty for Fielding to concern himself about, not least the threat of cholera spreading to the other wagons. To try and reduce the risk to the other families he had the Grants' and the major's wagons travel a discreet distance behind the rest of the train. John Grant drove his own wagon knowing that he too could fall foul of the disease at any time. Luke Hammond, an old-time friend of the major's volunteered to drive his team at great personal risk to himself. A couple of the other men rode as flankers to the two wagons to help in the event of trouble.

Late in the afternoon, as the train rolled on

across the flat prairie land below the Cimarron River, the reverend began to sense a change in the stiflingly hot weather. The mosquitoes and other biting insects that had accompanied them all the way west from Missouri disappeared from sight and the wind suddenly got up from the north. He pulled back strongly on the reins and brought his wagon to a standstill. The other wagons following on duly pulled up in line behind him.

'What's up, parson? Why have you stopped?' shouted Jake Clarke, whose wagon was next in line behind the minister's.

Fielding gazed all about him and sniffed the air expectantly. A hundred yards from the wagons a family of deer grazed contentedly, totally unconcerned about the strange vehicles that were crossing their range. On all sides of him the land lay flat and unmoving except for the parched, brown grass which swayed gently in the wind. Far off to the right of the train was a range of low hills bounded by a large number of trees. When he looked closer he immediately noticed the telltale signs of a big storm looming up from the north. It was still a long way off, but he knew it would hit the train before they made camp for the night. He looked back around the canvas cover of his wagon at Jake Clarke and pointed towards the distant hills. 'Storm's coming,' he said. 'We better find a good spot to hole up for the night while we can.'

Clarke gave him a wave. A moment later the wagons began to roll slowly forward in the direction of a small grove of cottonwood trees a few miles ahead.

A hundred yards behind the rest of them, the major tossed restlessly in a fever-racked sleep. If he had still been fit and active his finely honed instincts might have warned him of the imminent danger that lay in wait close by.

The Comanches lay stretched out still and low on their stomachs, hidden in the tall grass, with their ponies down beside them, watching the wagons from less than a quarter of a mile away. There were fifteen in the war party. Two of them were young boys on their first raid. Their main function was to guard the horses when an attack was made. The rest were experienced fighters who had taken many white and Mexican scalps. All shared a common desire to spill more white blood and return to their lodges with stories of brave deeds that would warm the hearts of the women and children.

The leader was an imposing figure of a man. His name was Scar. The old, jagged, inch-and-a-half-long battle wound on his left cheek had given him his name. In spite of the scar he was still a most handsome man. He had long, jet-black, greasy hair, dark eyes and a small mouth. Three eagle feathers adorned his head. At six foot two, he was unusually tall for a Kowadi Comanche. His wide-shouldered, lean, bronzed, muscular frame gave him an almost kingly appearance. At twenty-seven he was approaching his prime as a fighting warrior.

As the train passed by, Scar's attention fell on the two wagons trailing a hundred yards behind the rest. They aroused his curiosity. It seemed odd that they should court attack in such a fashion. But then he had long held the view that the whites were a very strange breed of people who did the most incredible things.

Scar beckoned his warriors in for a rapid council of war. As they knelt before him he explained the method of attack they would adopt. He ended the conference with a chopping motion of his hand at which point the Comanches unhobbled their horses, mounted swiftly and made off after the wagons.

The wagons were still some distance from the grove of cottonwoods when Scar's high-pitched, devilish war cry echoed across the land. The Comanches struck quickly and effectively, giving the men on the train no opportunity to support the isolated wagons which were carrying the cholera victims. Before anyone knew what was happening the warriors swept in from the rear and cut the two wagons off in an encircling movement that resembled the outstretched horns of a Texan steer.

The two outriders flanking the wagons were cut down in a hail of arrows. Before the drivers could react the warriors were aboard the wagons. Sharp-pointed knives gleamed in the afternoon sun and a moment later the drivers lay dead. A well-directed hatchet split the skull of the major before he could rise from his sick-bed to meet the attack.

The bodies of the two drivers were unceremoniously dumped out on the prairie as the whooping Comanches turned the wagons about and tore off at breakneck speed across the plains in the opposite direction to the main train.

Eight braves detached themselves from the fight and rode boldly forward to attack the main part of the train. They used the classic Comanche wheel method of attack, riding in just close enough to be able to send a volley of arrows and bullets at the travellers. The pilgrims dropped to the ground behind their wagons and returned fire. With each new charge the Comanches became ever bolder. They fired from beneath their ponies' necks, making it impossible for any of the defenders to pick a clear target.

The bitter exchange prevented any of the white folks from dashing to the support of the stolen wagons. It also provided covering fire for the two Comanches who were busy scalping the fallen drivers and outriders.

Scar finally gave the signal for the warriors to withdraw. They galloped off to catch up with the rest of the raiding-party. The defenders continued to fire long after the daring bucks had ridden way beyond the range of their guns.

From start to finish the attack had lasted no more than four minutes. A mood of abject depression and sorrow settled over the pilgrims. As they reclaimed their dead and laid them across the backs of four spare horses, a distant rumble of thunder confirmed the rapid approach of the storm.

Forty-five minutes later the wagon-train made camp for the night close to the grove of cottonwood trees that the reverend had wisely chosen for them. He made the families draw up their wagons in a tight circle right beside the narrow, shallow stream that meandered through the trees and out across the prairie. As soon as the circle was complete the menfolk all approached Fielding, anxious to hear what he had to say.

'The first thing we gotta do is get some hot food inside of us and then set up a guard rota,' advised

Henry Hemmings as they waited for Fielding to climb down from his wagon.

'Not the first thing,' replied the reverend sternly. The rebuke was delivered even before his feet touched the hard ground. 'Have you forgotten that some of our brethren are in need of burying?' His words immediately sank in. There was a murmur of agreement and much nodding of heads. Some of the men moved away to fetch shovels from their wagons while Fielding had the horses carrying the bodies of the fallen strapped to their backs brought forward.

Within a few minutes the entire population of the wagon-train had gathered on the banks of the tiny stream. As the men were laid to rest in narrow graves close to the grove of cottonwood trees the sky directly overhead began to rapidly darken. The air, which had been intensely hot and humid, soon turned cold and clammy. Little drops of rain fell from the sky to land with a steady, gentle, almost rhythmic plop, plop, on the heads of those gathered in a tight cluster beside the little stream. It was as if God himself was crying for the recently departed.

As the service got under way a great clap of thunder boomed out across the land. It drowned out some of the minister's words of comfort to the bereaved. Seemingly oblivious to the storm that was about to break directly overhead, he continued to read aloud from his bible. The young'uns and women looked up in fear towards the dark heavens. Another deafening peal of thunder was followed by a bright streak of forked lightning that came to earth some miles distant. But the men and the minister never once averted their eyes from the mounds of earth and simple wooden crosses that stood before them.

By the time Fielding had finished, the swirling, wind-driven black clouds had turned day to night. Even before the families started to move away towards the protection of their wagons the rain increased to monsoon proportions. It stung their faces and soaked their clothing. Instinctively they ran for cover, feeling certain that their dear, departed friends would forgive them for their seemingly indecent haste in seeking refuge from the deluge.

The storm raged about them for the best part of two hours. It frightened the children and spooked the livestock. Even when the thunder and lightning died away the rain continued to fall unabated long into the night. Fielding though was glad of the rain, for he was certain that it had saved the train from further Indian raids. Eating cold rations and catching up with a few stray horses and mules come morning was a small price to pay for their lives.

Like everyone else he eventually decided to turn in early and get a good night's sleep. As he settled down in the back of his cramped wagon he thought about the poor souls who had fallen into the Indians' hands. He had heard many tales of what the savages did to live captives and shuddered at the thought of what the victims had probably endured before finding relief in death. It troubled him greatly, but not as much as the realization that the people he was still responsible for could end up as further victims come morning. Such thoughts played on his mind and caused him to endure a fitful, uncomfortable sleep. Many others hunched up in the cramped, cold, leaking wagons suffered a similar fate that night.

FIVE

Fielding was already wide-awake when dawn broke. He pushed his cotton blanket aside and sat up in his makeshift bed in the wagon. When he reached for his black boots he found them to be still damp and muddy from the night before. They smelled to high heaven too, but he had no option but to pull them on. He rose from his cramped quarters, stretched his aching muscles and creaking joints, pulled back the flimsy, canvas flap at the rear of the wagon and exited via the tailgate.

Once his feet were safely on the ground he looked up into the dawn sky to behold the splendour of a world presided over by a canopy of pale blue and iridescent pink hues. Apart from a few white, wispy clouds the sky was clear. An enormous variety of birds were in fine song. Small drops of water in the grass sparkled and danced in the early morning light. It boded well for the day ahead.

A fine mist began to rise from the rain-soaked ground to drift easily away on the light westerly breeze. Everything seemed right with the world. The meadowlarks sang their song of welcome to the new day while the squirrels in the trees above his head chattered away incessantly to each other as they scampered about from branch to branch. It was all very reassuring, for the reverend was certain that had any Indians been prowling about the vicinity the various critters would not have been so chirpy and relaxed.

His feet produced a loud squelching sound as he set off to check on his flock. He didn't need any telling that the state of the ground would make it difficult for the train to make good progress. There was also every chance that some of the wagons would become bogged down in the ground when they tried to pull out.

People on the trail were often early risers, so he was not at all surprised to find a good many families already up and about when he made his rounds. All the menfolk gave him a friendly wave or a nod of the head as he passed by. Having completed his circumnavigation of the camp he returned to his wagon.

The travellers had a great deal of trouble in finding enough dry wood to build fires. A good deal of frustration and un-Godly cursing ensued before the men got their morning coffee. Fielding was halfway through his first cup of the day when Jake Clarke appeared at his shoulder. 'You figuring on pushing on after breakfast?' he asked, politely waving away Fielding's offer of coffee.

'Seems like the best thing to do,' replied the minister.

'You think the Indians will come back?'

Fielding sighed out loud and gazed across the land. 'I don't think so,' he replied. 'But as the major once told me, you can never take anything for granted.'

Clarke nodded, and tilted his damp, battered old hat a little further back over his head. 'How long do you figure it will be before we hit civilization?'

'No way of knowing for sure,' admitted Fielding, 'but I'll be mighty glad when I can hand over the responsibility for the train to someone more eminently qualified.'

His companion shot him a toothy, reassuring grin, exposing a set of black, rotting teeth. 'You're doing fine, reverend. We all got absolute faith in you.'

Fielding returned his smile. 'I know,' he replied, 'that's what's been bothering me!'

The fugitive soldiers rode right through the night. Hobbs had nothing but contempt for the inhabitants of the town and was certain they didn't possess the necessary courage or organization to mount a serious pursuit on their own. He also knew that it would take the best part of two days for the deputy to raise the alarm at Fort Walsh and for the army to respond to the situation. Even so, he didn't want to take any chances. By travelling fast and limiting their rest the sergeant figured they would put themselves beyond the reach of any patrol that was subsequently sent out after them.

When dawn broke the three men found themselves approaching a range of low, rolling hills. Small, scattered clusters of trees lined the base of the slopes.

Hobbs reined in his mount and eased himself out of the saddle to stretch weary limbs and knotted muscles. His equally tired companions were soon down at his side. The boy soldier, Baker, took his canteen from off his saddle-horn and drank what was left of the stale, tepid water that it contained. 'Where are we?' asked Cooper as he gazed about him to take in the country through which they were riding.

'Right slap-bang in the middle of Comanche country,' replied Hobbs as he crouched down on his haunches and toyed with a long blade of grass he had plucked casually from the ground.

'We'd best be moving on then,' said the kid in a tone of voice that suggested he was more than a little scared.

'Relax, boy,' replied Hobbs with a confident grin. 'The chances of us running into a Comanche war party are about as remote as you being able to find a good whore. This is a big country. Like as not we won't see hide nor hair of any Injun bucks all the way to the border.'

'Wish I felt as confident as you,' said Cooper, patting the neck of his mount.

'We'll be all right,' stated the sergeant, 'as long as we stay watchful and don't do anything stupid.'

'Which way do we go from here?' asked Cooper.

'We'll head south and skirt around the hills and then turn due west,' replied Hobbs, as he stood up and strolled towards his gently snorting horse. Without another word they remounted and rode off at a canter, keeping the hills to their right.

An hour later, as they started out across an area of flat, open, grassy country that stretched into the distance for as far as the eye could see, they caught sight of the unmistakable charred remains of two burnt-out wagons a quarter of a mile ahead of them. A number of misshapen bundles lay scattered haphazardly by one of the vehicles.

'What are they?' asked Baker, pointing at the still, grotesque shapes partly hidden in the grass.

'Bodies, kid,' replied Hobbs without a hint of sympathy for the victims.

'Comanches?' asked Cooper with an air of disgust.

'Most likely,' spat Hobbs.

'What are we going to do?' pressed Baker, his voice trembling with fear.

'Keep going,' said Hobbs simply.

'Are we going to bury them first?' queried Cooper.

'The hell we are,' retorted Hobbs. 'We ain't got the time. The raiding-party could still be somewhere close by. We got to ride.' Without another word the sergeant eased his mount forward, intent on giving the wagons a wide berth.

As they passed by the soldiers couldn't help but stare at the bodies in the grass. Baker almost retched on the rich, nauseating smell that wafted towards him on the morning breeze. For a while he couldn't get the thought of what the Comanches had done out of his mind.

Twenty minutes later they stumbled across the tracks of the wagon-train. The wheels of the heavily-laden wagons had flattened the grass and left shallow ruts in the ground which the overnight rain had filled. 'Looks like a good-sized train,' observed Hobbs, staring thoughtfully at the ground.

'Heading the same way we are too, I'd say,' added Cooper.

'Could be they might solve one or two of our problems for us.'

'How do you mean?'

'Food for one thing. We ain't eaten a decent meal in days and my stomach is sure complaining about it.'

Cooper grinned. 'Bet they've got some coffee too.'

'And a change of clothes for us. I'm tired of this blue. Never did sit my personality too well.'

'They might be willing to give us a meal if they think we're part of a patrol, but what kind of spiel are you going to give them to persuade them to let us have some civilian clothes?'

Hobbs spat on the ground. 'I ain't,' he said. 'We'll simply take what we want.'

'That'll cause trouble,' interrupted young Baker with genuine concern.

'We ain't on no picnic, kid,' replied Hobbs. 'Those people have what we need. If we're going to make it to Mexico we can't afford to be nice.'

'What if they fight?'

'We kill anyone who gets in our way, that simple.'

'Jesus, I don't know, sarge. Ain't we in enough trouble already?'

'God, kid, if you ain't one dumb son-of-a-bitch,' mocked Hobbs. Baker sought to avert his eyes from the sergeant's angry glare. 'We'll follow the tracks until we catch up with the pilgrims. Then we'll cadge a hot meal and when they lower their guard we'll take them by surprise and steal what we need.' His companions nodded in agreement. They rode west at a brisk canter, hoping to catch up with the wagons before the day was out.

* * *

The soft ground and distinctive marks of the cavalry-shod ponies made it easy for Kane to pick up the trail of the renegade troopers. 'If we keep pressing hard we should catch up with them by first light tomorrow morning,' he assured the other members of the posse.

'They got a good head start on us, Kane, you really think we can catch up so soon?' queried Brady.

'I'm sure,' replied Kane confidently. 'They'll have ridden through the night, but they can't keep that sort of pace up for too long. Once they figure themselves safe they'll start to ease up. As long as we limit our own rest we'll get them.'

'That's if the Comanches don't beat us to them,' advised York in a cautionary tone of voice.

Around noon they stopped by a narrow stream to eat and rest their mounts. The sun felt hot on their backs. There was hardly a cloud in the sky and only the lightest of breezes to keep the various flying insects at bay. The ground was rapidly drying out after the deluge of the night before. There was a freshness about the land. The grass seemed greener, where only hours earlier it had been more straw-coloured; the water-levels in the rivers and water-holes had been replenished; and the air itself was far less humid. They all knew though that within a matter of hours it would be as if the storm had never happened.

York took off his boots and socks and dangled his hot, smelly feet in the cooling waters of the stream. As he did so he noticed Kane quietly slipping into his saddle. 'Where are you going?' he asked.

'I want to take a look around,' came the reply. What he didn't reveal was that he had an uneasy feeling that they weren't alone. An in-built sixth sense kept telling him they were being watched.

A scout like Kane put great store in his instincts. It was what generally made the difference between life and death for a man in a harsh and unforgiving land where one mistake inevitably proved to be one too many. 'Stay put, I'll be back soon enough.'

He rode off at a trot away from the stream, first to the north and then, when he was out of sight of any prying eyes, he circled to the east. Within ten minutes he had cut the trail of a lone rider. The imprint of shod hooves told him the rider was a white man. Having studied the tracks he eased himself back into the saddle and set off back on a wide course to where the others were patiently waiting for him.

They were standing around chatting by their horses when he rode up. 'Well?' asked York, studying the scout's inscrutable face.

'We're being followed,' replied Kane.

'Comanches?'

'No, a white man.'

'Did you get close enough to see him?'

'No.'

'So how can you be sure he's white?'

'Shod horse.'

'Who do you think it is?' asked Brady, putting a gentle hand on the neck of Kane's horse.

'I'd say it's someone from town who wants in on the act,' replied Kane.

'What do we do?'

'Nothing ... for now. We'll just wait and see what he does.'

Brady nodded. With that they remounted and set off after the soldiers.

The wagons made good progress across the vast flat grassy prairie. By late afternoon they had covered close to eight miles, which was nearly as much ground as they had managed in a whole day when they were in the undulating country to the north of the Cimarron River.

Under normal circumstances the unchanging, featureless country would have seemed very tedious and boring to the families. However, with the ever present threat of further Indian attacks everyone was far too preoccupied with keeping their eyes open for boredom to become a possibility.

They still had four good hours of daylight left when Fielding was forced to call a premature halt to the day's journey. One of the rear wheels on Pete Forster's heavily over-loaded wagon finally gave way under the strain. The wagon and team were brought to a juddering, screeching halt.

'It'll take hours to repair,' announced Amos Grant as he stood beside the big Irishman and the reverend surveying the damaged wagon. He lifted his hat and scratched his balding head as Forster gave his wagon a bad-tempered kick.

'You can't say you weren't warned,' said Fielding, shaking his head in despair. 'The major told you this would happen.'

'I was robbed blind,' shouted Forster. 'The bloody wagon was worn-out when I bought it.'

'It's not the wagon, you darn fool, it's the amount of junk you have piled up inside of it,' said

Davy Arnold, who had the wagon right behind the Irishman's.

'Shut your mouth,' growled Forster. He was a gruff, unpleasant man at the best of times, but the loss of the wheel made him even meaner and more short-tempered than usual. Fielding shot Arnold a warning look as if to tell him to mind what he said. The last thing he needed was for the two men to have a wild set-to when there was work to be done.

'All right,' said Fielding. 'We'll camp here for the night. Once we've circled up we'll come and give you a hand.'

A short while later Fielding and a few others went to help Forster and his son replace the wheel. First they had to unload the entire contents of the wagon. 'Make sure you leave a lot of this junk behind when we pull out in the morning,' said Fielding. 'If you don't, not a man on this train will lift a hand to help you if you break down again.' Forster glared at the minister but wisely said nothing.

They found a thick branch to use as a lever to raise the wagon. Fielding, Grant and Arnold pulled down on the branch while Forster and sixteen-year-old Joey manoeuvred the wheel back into position. They had all but completed the back-breaking task when the branch snapped with a resounding crack that echoed out across the still prairie. The heavy wheel crashed down on top of Joey Forster's left leg. He screamed out in agony as the others raced to his side.

It took them a full minute to raise the wheel and release the boy. 'He's hurt bad,' shouted Arnold.

Fielding went down on one knee beside the boy and gently examined the leg while Pete Forster looked on anxiously. 'It's broken,' advised the minister.

Tears welled up in Pete Forster's eyes. He delicately cradled his son's head in his enormous, hairy hands. With a startled cry his pretty red-headed wife, Mary, came running from a neighbour's wagon to join them. The boy clenched his teeth against the intense pain in his leg. 'It's all right, son,' said Forster in the softest, most reassuring voice his wife had ever heard him use. 'You'll be fine, you'll see.'

'I've got to set the leg,' advised Fielding, looking into the big Irishman's eyes.

'Do you know how?'

'Yes. I've done it before. We never had a doctor of any sort during the war, so people quite naturally came to me for help. I was a quick learner.'

'All right,' said the big man, moving aside. 'But please try not to hurt him too much.'

The reverend nodded and patted him on the shoulder. 'Someone fetch me some short planks of wood.'

Arnold and Grant moved away to do his bidding. When they returned with a number of offerings he selected two suitable lengths for use as splints. He tore up an old shirt he was offered into strips to bind the splints to the boy's leg.

'This is going to hurt a mite, Joey, but only for a minute,' he warned, as he prepared to take hold of his leg. Joey just nodded and lay back. 'Take a tight hold on his arms.' Pete Forster and Davy Grant duly obliged. Joey cried out in pain as the reverend pulled his leg straight. Fielding then quickly and skilfully bound the splints into place like a seasoned frontier doctor.

When he had finished, Forster and Grant lifted the boy gently away from the damaged wagon to a place of safety. Mary stayed with her injured son while the menfolk returned to the task of fixing the wagon.

Once the wheel was securely back in place Mary left her friends to watch over her crippled son while she made a bed up for him in the back of the wagon. When she had finished the task her husband and Arnold lifted the boy slowly and carefully into the wagon.

'I'm obliged to you, Davy,' said Forster as they left Mary to care for the boy.

'You're welcome,' replied Arnold, shaking the Irishman's outstretched hand.

'I hope we can be friends from now on.'

'So do I.'

With that the two men parted company. Arnold returned to his own wagon while Forster went in search of Fielding. He found the reverend sitting on a large wooden box outside his wagon drinking coffee. The minister started to get up as the Irishman approached, but Forster waved him down. 'I had to come and say thank you for what you did for my boy.'

'Think nothing of it,' replied Fielding. 'Will you join me in a cup of coffee?'

'Gladly,' said Forster, seating himself cross-legged on a box at his side. 'You know, it ain't easy for a grown man to admit that he's been a damn fool.'

Fielding smiled as he handed the big man a cup

of coffee. 'Everyone makes mistakes. We can all be a little stubborn at times. I'm no different. I've done some darned fool things down the years that seemed right to me at the time.'

'It wouldn't have happened if I had listened to Peterson.'

'Maybe so. But feeling guilty won't help anything.'

The two men went on talking until they had emptied the entire contents of the minister's large enamel coffee-pot. By the time Forster took his leave of Fielding the big man felt much better about things. He knew he had made several new friends that day as a result of what had happened to his son.

No sooner was Fielding left alone than a cry went up from Tom Scott, one of the lookouts. Riders were approaching the camp. The minister instantly went to join him. Together they watched the three horsemen approach the camp. 'Well I'll be damned, it's the Cavalry!' exclaimed a disbelieving Scott. A huge smile of relief spread across both their faces.

SIX

The posse kept up their relentless pursuit of the deserters all through the long, hot afternoon. Hour after hour, mile after mile, they traversed the vast, seemingly endless, unchanging prairie without catching sight of another living soul. The burning-hot sun drained their energy and made it a most uncomfortable ride. Although the heat kept most of the mosquitoes at bay they were constantly attacked by large horseflies and the odd hornet. Every third hour they walked their horses for thirty minutes in order to conserve the animals' stamina for what lay ahead.

Late in the afternoon, when the shadows were beginning to lengthen, Kane spotted a number of large buzzards circling in the sky a mile or so ahead of them. He knew it meant trouble. 'Whoa,' he said, pulling back on his reins. He studied the waving sea of grass that stretched before him for as far as the eye could see.

'What's up?' asked Phillips, riding up alongside the scout.

'Something's either dead or in a pretty bad way,' he replied, pointing at the circling scavengers.

'Man or beast?' queried York with a worried frown.

'We'll find out soon enough,' said Kane, drawing his Winchester from the saddleboot alongside him. He set off at a brisk trot, leaving the others to trail behind.

Minutes later they found the grisly remains of the young family the soldiers had encountered earlier. The awful smell and pitiful sight of the bodies of the man, woman and two children caused Gannon and Brady to feel sick. Kane dismounted and carefully approached the stripped, bloodied and mutilated bodies. He pulled an arrow from the body of the nearest child. After scrutinizing the brightly-coloured bands on the shaft he discarded it and knelt down in the grass beside the body to examine the ground.

When he had finished he rose and walked over to the burnt-out remains of the prairie schooners. After the most cursory of inspections he returned to the other members of the group, ignoring the various items which lay scattered about in the grass.

'Comanches?' asked York with a pained expression on his face.

Kane nodded. 'Kowadis. Can tell by the markings on the arrows. Happened sometime late yesterday. I'd guess these two wagons became separated from a larger train and paid for the mistake with their lives.'

"Tis a savage land, Kane,' remarked Brady with a sad shake of his head.

'That it is,' replied Kane. 'At least for the unwary.'

'We'd best bury these poor unfortunate souls before we take up the chase,' said Phillips in a somewhat shaky voice. Kane nodded and went to

Bad Blood

fetch a shovel from one of the burnt-out wagons.

Three-quarters of an hour later they rode away having completed the unhappy task. Four simple wooden crosses atop low piles of rocks marked the pilgrims' last resting-place.

As the sun was about to sink beyond the western horizon they came upon the trail of the wagon-train. 'You figure they plan on joining up with the train?' asked Brady, as they sat astride their mounts studying the tracks.

'Most like,' replied Kane. 'If they do it will help us.'

'How come?'

'A wagon-train travels real slow, usually not much more than ten or twelve miles a day. If they tie in with them we'll overtake them all the sooner.'

'How long 'til they catch up with the wagons?' asked York.

'Soon.'

'What about us?'

'If we ride until full dark, snatch a few hours sleep and then set out again around midnight, we should catch up by noon tomorrow.'

'Then we have them bang to rights,' announced Phillips, slapping his thigh in excitement.

'Don't count your chickens,' warned Kane. 'We still have a lot of hard riding to do. Besides which the Comanches might well be after the train too.'

'You think it likely?' asked Gannon.

'I'd say so,' said Kane. 'They'd see those pilgrims as easy pickings.'

'Then is it wise to be travelling at night? We could ride slap-bang into an ambush,' said Phillips. From the tone of his voice it was obvious that he didn't exactly relish the prospect of fighting a parcel of angry savages in the dark.

'Comanches don't fight at night,' stated Brady confidently.

'The hell they don't,' corrected Kane. 'A Comanch' will fight you anytime and anywhere the urge grabs him. They particularly favour an attack when the moon's up.'

The smug look quickly disappeared from Brady's face. 'Then how come it's accepted as gospel by most folks that Indians don't attack at night?'

Kane shook his head as if in pity for the man's stupidity. 'Most folks don't get close enough to the Comanche to know 'em well enough to be sure of anything. But I know 'em, and I'm telling you, if you go by any such assumption then likely as not it'll cost you your hair one day.'

'And knowing that, you'd still have us ride through the night?' queried Phillips.

'We have to,' said Kane. 'Otherwise we'll never catch up to 'em.'

'Well how do we make sure we don't end up as buzzard-meat?'

'Don't worry, Phillips, I don't aim to have my hair dangling from any Comanche lance if I can avoid it.'

'Kane knows the country, and he knows Comanches,' advised York. 'He'll see us all right.'

The veteran trooper looked from one anxious face to another. Eventually they all nodded in turn. Kane spurred his horse forward at a walk, keeping the wagon tracks to his left. The others fell into step behind him.

As the last pink rays of twilight gave way to full

dark Kane called a halt. He insisted on a cold camp for fear of alerting any prowling Comanches to their presence. Any young buck worth his salt could see or smell a cooking-fire from miles away. They ate cold rations of hardtack and beans before stretching out for a few hours' rest.

Kane stood the first watch. The breeze was just sufficient to keep most of the annoying, bloodsucking insects at bay. But the night still felt uncomfortably hot and close. Far off, a coyote howled its welcome to the moon. A short distance away a diamond-back rattlesnake slithered through the tall grass in search of a much needed meal.

Just as he was beginning to enjoy his spot of night duty Kane became aware of a sudden, unnatural movement way off to his right. He froze to the spot, fully alert and ready for action. Seconds later he saw a crouching, fast-moving shape heading towards the camp.

Slowly and silently Kane eased himself behind the boulder he had been resting against. Hardly daring to breathe for fear of divulging his position he watched the dark shadow draw closer. As soon as the man went past him the scout slipped around the far side of the boulder and came up behind him.

Their uninvited guest had his rifle at his shoulder when Kane's intimidating voice broke the silence. 'If I was you I'd throw the gun down and turn around with your hands up.'

The man froze. For a moment Kane thought he was going to obey, but then the figure spun round, gun at the ready. Both men seemed to fire as one. Kane was marginally quicker on the trigger. His bullet sent the man spinning away backwards to the ground.

Everyone in camp came awake with a start. They jumped to their feet and ran to Kane's side. By the time they reached him he was already squatting over the body. Kane turned the man over onto his back and stared into the lifeless eyes of Tom Harmer.

'Isn't that the guy who was so determined to see us hung?' asked York.

'Yep,' replied Brady sadly. 'That's Tom Harmer all right.'

'Damn fool,' muttered Kane. 'I gave him every chance to put his gun down.'

'Must've been him that was following us,' said Halliday. 'He just couldn't accept the fact that we had nothing to do with killing his nephew.'

'That's the way it looks to me,' agreed Phillips.

'Let's get the hell out of here,' urged Kane. 'Sound carries a long way at night. If there are any Comanches about they sure as hell know where we are now.'

'So much for a few hours' shut-eye,' said Gannon reflectively.

'We can rest up later,' promised Kane. 'Now let's throw Harmer over his horse and get out of here.'

Kane set out to find the dead man's horse while the others broke camp and saddled up. They were just about ready to leave by the time he returned with Harmer's nervous pinto pony. No one said a word as the scout led them off at a canter across the moonlit prairie.

Some thirty minutes later Kane decided it was safe to rest up for a few more hours. He found a small grove of cottonwoods that offered good cover in the unlikely event of any wandering Comanches stumbling across their trail.

'Two hours, maybe three, then I want us back in the saddle,' he said as they dismounted. 'York, it's your watch. Wake Gannon in an hour so that he can take over from you.' The trooper drew his carbine from his saddleboot and went and stood by the edge of the trees. Within minutes the others had settled themselves down to snatch what little sleep they could.

A welcoming committee had formed by the time the soldiers trotted their horses into the circle of wagons. 'My name is Thomas Fielding,' said the reverend, stepping forward to introduce himself with an extended hand. 'Won't you step down and join us in a little supper?'

'Don't mind if we do,' replied Hobbs, reaching down to shake hands. 'Sergeant Hobbs, 5th United States Cavalry, out of Fort Walsh. A fella could mistake you for a man of the church from the cut of your dress.'

'That is precisely what I am. And at present I am also the leader of this band of Christian folk.'

'Well I'll be darned!' said Hobbs with an amused smile on his face.

'You might say I had the burden of command thrust upon me in unfortunate circumstances,' replied Fielding.

'We were heading south when we cut your trail some miles back. Knowing there are Comanches in the area we thought we'd look you over and make sure you were all right,' explained Hobbs, while his two companions explored the eager, welcoming faces.

'That was right thoughtful of you, sergeant,' said Fielding. He went on to describe their run-in with the Comanches the day before.

'Then I'm sure glad we decided to check you out. Maybe we can ride with you a ways? At least until we are certain the danger is truly behind you.'

'We'd all be grateful for that,' confessed Fielding, to a murmur of agreement from the crowd. 'Now why don't you gentlemen unsaddle your mounts and come eat with us?'

The soldiers didn't need any second invitation. They admitted that they hadn't eaten proper food in so long it was doubtful if their stomachs would know what it was. A general ripple of laughter greeted their response.

After supper Hobbs offered to take a turn around the defences. Cooper and Baker went with him. 'Well?' asked Cooper, when they were out of earshot of anyone on the train.

'Well what?' queried Hobbs as he came to a standstill just outside the circle of wagons.

'What the hell do we do now? That's what.'

'Take it easy, keep your voice down,' instructed an angry-looking Hobbs.

'Just answer the question,' said Cooper in a lower voice.

'Have you noticed how heavy these wagons are travelling?' replied Hobbs, jabbing a finger back over his shoulder at the circle right behind them.

'So what? It ain't no great surprise,' said Cooper. 'Pilgrims always pack everything they possibly can into their wagons.'

'Including all their gold,' stated Hobbs with a wicked glint in his eye.

'You're crazy,' said Cooper, trying very hard to keep his voice down. 'These people ain't got no gold.'

'How do you know that? You asked 'em?'

'Hell no, Hobbs, you only got to look at them. These are dirt-farmers. They lost any money they had in taxes when the carpet-baggers moved in at the end of the war. You must know that?'

'I don't know any such thing,' the sergeant replied, spitting on the ground. 'Never yet met a man who tried to make a fresh start without a little money to back him up.'

'I thought all we wanted was a little food and a change of clothes?' interceded Baker anxiously.

'Shut up, kid,' snapped Hobbs. 'We're gonna need us a stake in Mexico. I reckon we might as well get it now.'

'I don't like it,' said Baker.

'You better mind me, boy,' growled Hobbs contemptuously. 'Any more of your foolishness and I swear I'll leave your bones for the vultures to feast on.'

Baker averted his eyes and swallowed hard. Not for the first time he regretted his bold, hasty, ill-conceived notion to follow Hobbs. 'So what are we gonna do?' asked Cooper.

Hobbs paused and then scowled at Baker before replying. 'We spend the night with these good Christian folk. Then come morning we get the drop on them and relieve them of all the money they're carrying.'

'And some civilian clothes,' Cooper added.

'Yeah,' agreed Hobbs with a nod of his head.

'How do you plan to get the money?'

'I ain't exactly formulated a plan yet. But I'll

think of something, never you fear. Just take your cue from me when the time comes. That goes for you too, kid, or I swear I'll put a bullet through that stupid skull of yours.'

Baker flashed him an angry look but wisely chose not to back it up with hasty words. 'The kid'll do fine, you'll see,' said Cooper.

'He better,' replied Hobbs aggressively. He then led them back to the protection of the wagons.

Just as twilight settled over the plains, something quite spontaneous and totally unexpected happened within the camp. As the shadows lengthened and the flames of a dozen small fires began to take on greater definition in the failing light, someone started to play a familiar tune on an old fiddle. Almost immediately the catchy, foot-tapping melody was taken up by a neighbour on his squeeze-box. Next, a number of young, happy, excited voices broke into song, which encouraged others, seated around their camp-fires, to clap along in rhythm.

In the twinkling of an eye, Henry Mathison took his wife Bertha by the hand and began to dance in front of their wagon to great applause from their neighbours. Within minutes children, who had been put to bed right after supper, came tumbling out of the wagons to join them. They were immediately followed by a growing number of adults.

Soon it was just like a regular, old-fashioned hoedown back home. The music, singing and hand-clapping got steadily louder and louder. At one point it seemed as if every couple on the train had joined the Mathisons. The dancers whirled and twirled their way about the inner circle with big, beaming smiles on their trail-dirty faces. The flickering flames of the fires within the circle danced a pattern of their own, casting a warm red and yellow glow over the happy folk, who had momentarily forgotten all about the troubles they had recently endured.

Fielding leaned against the tailgate of his wagon and watched the fun with a contented smile on his face. It was a wonderful sight. The shadows of the dancers moved constantly to and fro against the backdrop of the canvas sides of the wagons.

For a moment he lifted his head and gazed into the darkening heavens. The moon was up. All about, a thousand stars sparkled and twinkled. He watched as a shooting-star flared brightly and then died as it completed its voyage across the deep, inky-blue sky. It was a most reassuring spectacle.

'They've forgotten what's out there,' observed Davy Arnold as he strolled to the reverend's side.

Fielding turned his head and smiled pleasantly at his good friend. 'I was so preoccupied I never even heard you arrive,' said the minister.

'Some wagon-master you are!' joked Arnold, as the two men stood side by side watching the revellers enjoy themselves.

'It doesn't take much for people to forget, does it?'

'No, it sure don't.'

'Who's standing watch?'

'Art Tambling and his son. I think I'll go check on 'em. Might even spell him a while so he can join in the fun.'

'His wife won't thank you any,' advised

Fielding. 'Sue says he's the worst dancer south of the Mason-Dixon line. He's always treading on her feet.' Arnold laughed and gave him a dismissive wave of his hand as he hurried on his way.

'Well, I do declare, it's a regular hoedown,' observed Cooper as he pushed back the thick saddle-blanket that was draped over him.

'This could be just the chance we've been waiting for,' said Hobbs, coming to his feet. His scheming mind was working overtime. The general fatigue and aching in his joints vanished in a trice. He went into a hushed conference with his accomplices.

Once he had briefed them, they all split up and slunk away to search the wagons for concealed valuables. The task of searching the wagons proved more difficult and time-consuming than any of them had figured. Moving around the cramped interiors of the wagons was hard enough, but having to do it in the dark made it all but impossible to locate the trunks and secret places where any money would have been hidden away. In the end they gave it up as a bad job. 'Well, with all this ruckus going on we ain't gonna get much sleep,' said Hobbs, 'so we might as well go and join in the fun.'

The soldiers moved off to join the happy crowd. They halted on the edge of the improvised dance-floor and joined in the clapping and cheering. Baker became aware of a tall, blonde, green-eyed filly who was standing just a few feet away with a mischievous look on her happy young face. She kept coyly glancing in his direction, but for never more than a second at a time. 'Seems to me she wants you, kid,' said Cooper, digging his young companion in the ribs with his elbow.

'Get out of here,' retorted the young soldier, flushing with embarrassment.

'I tell ya, kid, she's flaunting herself at ya. Go ahead, ask her for a dance.'

Before Baker had a chance to reply, the girl in question, egged on by one of her friends, moved gracefully to his side. 'I ain't never danced with a soldier before,' she said, looking him directly in the eye. When he looked away, unsure of how to respond, she blushed slightly but made no effort to move on.

'Go ahead, kid,' said Cooper good-naturedly, 'it's high time you grew up.'

'What's the matter, don't you like me?' she teased.

'It ain't that,' replied Baker nervously.

A quizzical look appeared on her attractive, tanned face. 'Why won't you dance then?'

'I don't know how,' he replied, averting his eyes and shuffling his feet.

'Then I'll just have to teach you,' she said, grabbing hold of his hand. She dragged the embarrassed young trooper out into the middle of the improvised dance-floor just as the fiddler prepared to strike up a new tune.

When the music started she guided him through the rudimentary steps of a traditional folk-dance. He felt very self-conscious, fearing that everyone was watching his clumsy attempts to follow his partner without stepping on her dainty little feet. He felt certain he would trip over his own feet and end up flat on his back before the dance ended. But his fears proved to be groundless, for he was still standing when the fiddler ceased his playing and accepted the generous applause of the crowd.

They stood gawking at each other for a few seconds then she gently squeezed his hand and smiled the warmest, prettiest smile he had ever seen in his entire life. 'You're mighty pretty,' he said. He hadn't meant to say it, but somehow the words just popped right out. The girl blushed and then giggled. 'What's your name?' he asked.

'Nancy. What's yours?'

'Daniel. Daniel Baker.'

'Well, Daniel Baker, come and meet my folks.' She promptly dragged him off to meet her parents.

'Looks like the kid's done all right for himself,' joked Cooper, as he watched the happy teenagers slip away.

'Reckon he has,' replied Hobbs with a grin. 'Now it's my turn.'

'Is that wise?' queried Cooper with a worried frown. 'There ain't likely to be any unattached females of our age on this here train.'

'What does that matter?' retorted Hobbs. 'I reckon these folks should be more than willing to show their gratitude for the army putting in an appearance to save their miserable hides.'

Cooper grabbed hold of him by the arm. 'It'll cause trouble,' he warned.

Hobbs pulled Cooper's hand away. 'Don't worry,' he said. 'All I'm gonna do is have a little fun, that's all.'

The sergeant moved away in the direction of a bevy of young ladies who were laughing amongst themselves beside one of the numerous fires that

Bad Blood

glowed ever more brightly in the night. 'Well now,' he said in a friendly tone of voice, 'which one of you gals is gonna give this here sergeant a dance?'

There were no takers. None of them fancied strutting out with a man who was old enough to be their father. Maybe if he hadn't stunk to high heaven and looked an utter mess to boot one of them might have done the neighbourly thing and met his request.

'Well, have ya got manners or ain't ya?' he bellowed, frightening the life out of them.

'Our folks don't like us going with strangers,' replied one of the girls with a sharp edge to her voice.

'I ain't no stranger, girls, I'm more like everyone's favourite uncle,' he said, laughing at his own joke. When no one responded to his continued advances he stepped forward and roughly grabbed the nearest girl by the arm. 'You'll damn well dance with me and like it,' he snapped, pushing her towards the revellers. The girl squealed and struggled against his vice-like grip. Immediately two determined figures suddenly loomed up menacingly in front of him. Both had rifles pointed in his direction.

'We don't take kindly to anyone thrusting their attention on our young women,' announced Jim Fraser, who happened to be a close friend of the girl's father. 'Now unhand her.'

For a moment Hobbs stood stock-still, making no effort to release his painful grip on the girl. He instinctively flexed the fingers of his free hand over the flap that hid his army revolver. But going for his gun wasn't a serious option, not with two unwavering rifles centred on his midriff. 'All I wanted was one lousy dance,' he growled as he angrily pushed the girl away from him.

'You should have asked proper,' rebuked Fraser, with a dead-pan face. 'Now be on your way.'

'You ain't heard the last of this,' warned Hobbs, under his breath, as he turned on his heels and strode away. It was then that two gunshots rang out, loud and clear, in quick succession. Everyone within the circle of wagons instantly froze and a deathly silence settled over the camp.

SEVEN

Within minutes of leaving Fielding, Arnold found Jason Tambling standing watch by his parents' wagon. Arnold stopped beside him and laid a reassuring hand on the eighteen-year-old's shoulder. 'Any sign of trouble?' he asked casually, as he took in the boy's field of vision.

'No,' came the reply. 'Everything's as still and quiet as a graveyard, 'cept for the dancing of course.'

'Glad to hear it,' grinned Arnold. 'Where's your pa at?'

'He should be at the other end of the camp,' replied Jason.

'Mmm,' said Arnold, 'I'm surprised I didn't see him on my way over.'

'Pa has a habit of doing his watching from the prairie itself,' stated Jason good-naturedly.

'That must be why I missed him,' said Arnold. He quickly made his way to the opposite side of the camp, taking care to keep clear of the dancers.

Art Tambling was nowhere to be seen. Arnold decided to step outside the circle in search of him. He had gone about thirty yards when some sixth sense caused him to halt. The hair on the back of his neck started to stand on end, his heart began to beat at a faster rate and a cold chill ran down his spine. Although he couldn't explain it, he knew something was terribly wrong.

For a moment he contemplated calling out to try and locate his friend, but then he thought better of it. His sharp, darting eyes revealed nothing in the vicinity to explain his unease. He listened intently to what the night had to say, still hoping that his friend would materialize out of the dark. But it didn't happen.

The night was unnaturally still and quiet. There was no symphony of chirping crickets, or song of the night-birds, or coyote howls. It could only mean that the critters of the night had been disturbed.

The palms of his hands felt cold and clammy. Fear, of the genuine, muscle-binding, mind-numbing kind, coursed through his body. It prevented him from either shouting out a warning to those back on the train or from taking to his heels. He jerked his head to the left in response to the unexpected call of a whip-poor-will out there in the grass. Almost at once the call was answered from the darkened prairie far off to his right.

In the darkness the Comanches were slowly and cautiously moving in, hoping to cut him off from his line of retreat. He knew there was nothing he could do to help Tambling. His one hope was that his friend had not been taken alive.

Arnold was on the verge of panic. His whole body seemed to be shaking uncontrollably. Goose-pimples appeared on his lower arms. Swallowing hard, he forced himself to think things out calmly and rationally. Safety lay tantalizingly just a short distance behind him, but he resisted the temptation to make a dash for it. He knew that any sudden movement on his part would only have brought him an arrow in the back. But he couldn't remain where he was indefinitely, not with an unknown number of savages gradually tightening the net on him.

He dropped to one knee and pretended to look for sign, half expecting to hear the telltale whoosh of an arrow through the air. When none came he breathed a deep sigh of relief. It seemed that the Comanches were in no hurry to end the game they were playing. He stood up again, looked all about him, and started off slowly to the left in the general direction of the first whip-poor-will call.

Every few yards he paused and pretended to inspect the ground at his feet. Each time he moved off again he slightly angled his line of march, so that he gradually drew closer to the circle of wagons. He was only twenty yards from the wagons when he stumbled across the body of Art Tambling. His friend's throat had been cut. A bloody bald patch on the top of his head glistened in the moonlight where they had paused to take his scalp. His firearms were gone.

The discovery sent Arnold's head spinning. For a moment he thought he was going to be sick. He knew it was highly unlikely he would make it back to the wagons alive. Too many unseen Comanche bows were already trained on him. They had him dead to rights. But if he was to die he resolved to take a few of them with him.

He took a deep breath, cocked the hammer of his pistol and came to his feet on the run. His zigzag dash had taken him barely six yards before two arrows swished through the still night air to cut him down. He cried out in pain and fell to the ground with an arrow embedded in his lower back.

As he lay there on his side, struggling to catch his breath, fighting back the paralysing wave of agony that surged through him, he became aware of a number of dark shapes looming up out of the prairie. He watched their approach out of the corner of his eye. A short, bandy-legged young buck was the first to reach him. He was little more than a boy, inexperienced in the dangerous art of warfare. The excitement of his first kill glowed in his black eyes. He stood over the prostrate body and grinned in satisfaction at his handiwork. With a muted whoop he fell on his quarry and sat with his legs straddling him. He made a grab for the long, wavy brown hair with his left hand.

It was the moment Arnold had been waiting for. He had stubbornly refused to give up his slender hold on life until one or more of the Comanches were close enough for him to indulge himself in one last act of defiance. As the foolish young Comanche tightened his grip, Arnold's eyes flashed open. The savage gave a startled cry and withdrew his knife. Before he could react Arnold shot him in the chest at point-blank range.

The dead Comanche toppled backwards away from him. Arnold fanned back the hammer of his pistol, sat up, coughed painfully once, and, ignoring the blood that flowed freely from his mouth, he fired at the nearest Comanche. The bullet hit the warrior in the shoulder, shattering the bone.

Before Arnold could get off another shot three more Comanches hurtled forward and fell on him.

Their knives flashed in the moonlight as they cut and slashed at him until he lay motionless on the ground. With a sickening, tearing sound one of them prised his scalp from his head and gleefully held it aloft for the others to see. They quickly disappeared into the night knowing that the white man's unexpectedly tough resistance had cost them the element of surprise.

The stunned silence within the compound lasted but a few seconds. A woman screamed, the menfolk looked anxiously at one another and then the powerful voice of the Reverend Fielding boomed out a sequence of short, urgent instructions. 'Douse those camp-fires. Get your guns. Man the perimeter. Women and children get under cover, right now!'

Instantly the frozen tableau became a frenzied, frightened hive of activity. Steam rose from the fires and vanished into the night sky as buckets of water were hurriedly poured onto the flames to kill the silhouettes of those within the defensive circle. The women and children huddled together in fear in the centre of the compound beside the livestock. Some of the young ones were crying. 'Quit your wailing,' yelled Hobbs, at one and all, as he hurried by on his way to find the reverend.

He found him kneeling down by the wheel of his wagon surveying the still prairie beyond. 'Can't see a darned thing,' said Fielding, after nodding a welcome in the sergeant's direction.

'That's when they're at their most dangerous, when you can't see 'em,' advised Hobbs. 'Who fired the shots?'

'Can't be sure, but I'd guess it was either Art Tambling or Davy Arnold. It appears they're both unaccounted for.'

'You mean they're both dead,' corrected Hobbs, very matter-of-factly.

The sergeant had no sooner spoken than a flaming arrow appeared in the sky. They watched mesmerized as it arced its way towards them. It fell harmlessly inside the circle and was immediately stamped on by the nearest of the defenders. Others were not long in coming. One fell a fraction short, but two others hit their intended targets. Instantly, the canvas covers of two wagons a short distance from the reverend's caught alight. The reaction of the defenders was swift and effective. Half a dozen men grabbed buckets of water and immediately set about putting out the flames.

'Are they going to keep this up all night?' asked Fielding, the frustration in his voice clear for all to hear.

'No,' replied Hobbs. 'Right now they're just feeling us out. There's much worse than this to come.'

'Come on, you red devils, and let's be done with it,' screamed an angry voice from one of the other wagons.

As if to honour his request the Comanches suddenly appeared as fast-riding, ghostly shadows forty yards from the wagons. They whooped and yelled at the top of their lungs as they circled the wagons firing from under their horses' necks. Instantly a dozen guns within the compound returned fire. Just as quickly as they had appeared, the raiders melted back into the darkness.

Everything fell strangely quiet once more. It was as if the Comanches had never been there. 'Anybody hurt?' asked Fielding anxiously.

Several voices, one after the other, assured him that the defenders had suffered no casualties. 'Keep watch,' said Hobbs, 'I'm gonna check out the rest of the circle.'

'You think they'll come again?' asked Fielding, as the sergeant made to leave.

'You can count on it,' replied Hobbs over his shoulder, as he went in search of his fellow troopers.

Cooper was lying flat on his belly beneath one of the wagons. He had his rifle poised at his shoulder and his eyes trained on the prairie. Hobbs stood behind him and kicked him none too gently in the leg to announce his presence. The trooper turned angrily, but instantly relaxed when he recognized the protuberant frame of the sergeant. 'Where's Baker?' growled Hobbs, as Cooper rose from the ground to stand beside him.

'Last time I saw him he was talking with the parents of his new girlfriend,' he replied, leaning the stock of his rifle on the ground.

'Go find him,' ordered Hobbs with a scowl. 'I'll wait here for you.'

Cooper found the young trooper sitting on the ground talking to Nancy by the tailgate of her folks' wagon. 'Sergeant needs us,' he explained, doffing his hat at the girl.

'OK,' replied Baker. He turned and smiled at the frightened girl at his side. 'Don't worry, Nancy, I'll be back presently,' he assured her. She smiled back somewhat nervously and gave him a short little wave as he left with Cooper.

They found Hobbs exactly where Cooper had left him. 'We gotta get out of here,' announced Hobbs, glancing all about to see if anyone was watching them.

'We can't, sarge, these people need us,' pleaded Baker, looking towards Cooper for support.

The sergeant grabbed hold of the youth firmly by the front of his dirty blue tunic, forcing him up onto his toes. He put his head right into his startled face. 'Damn these dirt-scratchers, boy. We ain't interested in no one's hide but our own. Now you just shut your mouth and heed me.'

Baker, scared witless by the sergeant's unexpected outburst and his ever tightening grip on his personage, nodded and made an effort to ground his heels.

'You ain't fixin' to ride out while those Comanch' are still about, are ya?' asked Cooper.

'I sure am,' replied Hobbs, releasing Baker. 'What better time to leave than when the Comanch' will be keepin' these pilgrims busy?'

'But how do we get through them?' pressed Cooper doubtfully.

'Hell, you're more trouble than Baker. How long you been in the territory, Cooper?'

'Since the end of the war.'

'And you still don't know nothin' 'bout Comanches, that's for sure.'

'What do ya mean?'

'Tell me, what are you expecting the Comanch' to do next?'

'They'll probably hit us a few more times while the moon's up, then wait until dawn and come in hard.'

'Exactly,' replied Hobbs. 'The only thing I like about the Comanches is their predictability. Now if it were Kiowas that were out there it would be an all too different mess of pigs, they always do what you least expect.'

'So how does that help us?' interrupted Baker, on regaining a small measure of confidence.

'The way it helps us, dumb-ass,' sneered Hobbs, 'is that once they settle down, sometime after midnight, they won't be expecting anyone on the train to make a break for it. And that is precisely what we'll do. Before they know what's happened we'll be through them and away.'

'What if they chase us?' argued Cooper.

'They won't,' Hobbs assured him confidently. 'They'll be more interested in the loot they can gain from the train come morning.'

'Why don't we just stay with the train all the way to New Mexico?' suggested Baker. He didn't much like the idea of riding through a parcel of Comanches in the dark. It scared him even more than the thought of standing up to the bullying sergeant.

'Christ, kid, you just ain't got no brains, have ya? If we stay with the train, sooner or later the army or the law will catch up with us for sure. I'd rather take my chances with the Comanches any day than end up with a rope round my neck.'

'I think you might have a point there, sarge,' agreed Cooper. Hobbs raised his eyebrows in the direction of the kid. He nodded slowly in acquiescence.

'That's better,' said Hobbs happily. 'Now, I've got a pretty good plan worked out to get the money and clothes we came for.'

'Go on,' urged Cooper, when the sergeant hesitated for a moment.

'About an hour or so before dawn we'll grab ourselves a couple of hostages. That way the reverend and his flock will have to lay down their guns and let us take what we want.'

'Might just work,' agreed Cooper.

'Ain't no might about it,' replied Hobbs with a grin. 'We collect up all their guns, wait 'til they hand over all their money and the clothes we need, and then we just ride out hell for leather with the hostages along for good measure.'

'You can't ride off with their guns. They'll have nothing to defend themselves with against the Indians,' said Baker in a voice that was dangerously above that of a whisper.

'Keep your voice down, boy!' exclaimed Hobbs. 'You'll alert the whole train.'

'I don't care,' replied the trooper defiantly, but in a lowered voice. 'It just ain't right to leave them without guns.'

'He has a point,' agreed Cooper.

The sergeant looked from one to the other of them. After taking a few seconds to think things over he said, 'All right.' Then he shook his head as if he was going against his better judgement. 'All right, we leave them their guns. We just empty all the bullets out of them and throw them down on the ground when we leave.' His companions nodded in agreement.

'Do you have any particular hostages in mind?' asked Cooper.

'Any one of the kids will do,' advised Hobbs. 'Along with Baker's young fancy piece.'

'No,' snapped Baker, clearly angered by the suggestion.

'Thought you'd be glad to have her along,' joked Hobbs.

'Well I ain't. I don't want her touched.'

'You ain't got no say in the matter,' said Hobbs. 'If I hear any more objections I might just put a bullet in her brain before we leave.'

'I want your promise that no harm'll come to her,' said Baker, knowing there was no way he could stop Hobbs taking the girl with them.

'You have my word, kid. I swear it on my mother's grave.' The smirk on the man's face did little to instil confidence in Baker that the promise would be lived up to, but he still nodded in agreement. 'OK,' said Hobbs, keeping his voice low. 'Now go back to where you were stationed and wait 'til I come get ya.'

When the moon was at its zenith the Comanches mounted a series of lightning raids which lasted for the best part of three hours. Although they suffered no casualties, the nerves of the defenders became increasingly frayed. Around three in the morning the sporadic raids finally stopped. Things remained still and quiet for nearly an hour, until a sudden, unexpected volley of fire-arrows provoked a frantic bout of activity within the circle. 'They're just trying to make sure we don't catch any sleep,' advised Hobbs, as he strolled over to where Fielding was standing surveying the scene. 'They want to make sure we ain't fresh and sharp when they come for us in the morning.'

'We'll still give them a darned good fight,' Fielding promised.

'I'm gonna check on my troopers,' said Hobbs. 'I'll be back presently.' The reverend gave him a nod as the sergeant turned his back and set off in search of his companions.

He found them standing guard on the far side of

camp. 'All right now, listen,' said Hobbs as they all went down on one knee. 'Baker, you go fetch your girl, and be quick about it.'

'What do I tell her?' he asked nervously.

'Anything you damn well like, just bring her here.' The boy nodded and set off towards Nancy's wagon. 'You and me are gonna go get ourselves a young'un,' added Hobbs to Cooper when the boy had left. With that they walked side by side to where all the children were stretched out on the ground, trying to sleep, on the far side of the livestock.

Cooper carefully approached a young boy who was lying down with his back to the soldiers. Before the youngster knew what was happening, Cooper was kneeling beside him with a hand clasped tightly over his mouth. The boy struggled and kicked out wildly as he was lifted to his feet. But although he fought like a tiger he was just too small to make any impression on his captor. The trooper dragged him backwards to the pre-arranged rendezvous with Baker.

'What's going on? What are you doing with little Billy Burrows?' asked Nancy with a worried frown when she saw the boy was trying to resist the rough hold Cooper had on him.

'Shut up,' growled Hobbs. He stepped towards her and twisted her arm up behind her back. 'If you say another word I'll break your arm.'

The frightened girl knew he meant it. She managed to stifle the cry that was about to escape her throat. 'You promised not to hurt her,' said Baker urgently, while trying to step in between Nancy and the sergeant.

'I won't, so long as she does as she's told. Now

bind her hands and be quick about it.'

Baker didn't like it, but he did as he was told. He then went over and did the same to their other little hostage while Cooper kept a tight grip on his arms. The youngster redoubled his efforts to fight off his captor. He stamped painfully down on Cooper's right foot and at the same time managed to open his mouth wide enough to bite the hand that covered it. The soldier withdrew his hand and let out a yell at the same time that the boy screamed for help.

Hobbs moved across to where the boy was standing, shouting his head off. He back-handed him hard across the face, knocking him to the ground. Reaching down he hauled the kid back to his feet by his shirt-front. 'Try that again, kid, and I'll bend the barrel of my gun over yer head. Understand?'

The terrified youngster just nodded as tears welled up in his eyes. He was made to stand next to Nancy. The soldiers sheltered behind them with their pistols drawn. All about them people were racing to the scene.

A tall, balding man with questioning eyes was the first to arrive. He stopped suddenly less than six yards away, brought up short by the sight of the gun pointed in his direction by the bulky, unsmiling sergeant. 'What the hell's going on here?' he demanded in a raised voice that carried throughout the length and breadth of the compound. 'What are you doing with my boy?'

'If you want your kid back in one piece don't come any closer,' warned Hobbs. The rest of the crowd halted in line with Frank Burrows and looked at each other in puzzled fashion.

Amy Burrows jostled her way through the throng of people and wrapped herself inside the protective arms of her husband. 'Oh, Frank, don't let him hurt our Billy,' she pleaded. Tears began to trickle down her cheeks.

'He ain't gonna hurt anyone, I promise you, woman.' The calm, determined voice of Frank Burrows didn't faze the arrogant sergeant in the least. He stood unwaveringly in front of the crowd with his gun levelled pointedly at Frank Burrows. 'You touch one hair on that boy's head and you're a dead man,' promised the angry father with a sibilant quality to his voice.

'Easy, Frank,' said Fielding, pushing his way to the front so that he could act as mediator. 'Why don't you tell us what all this is about?' he suggested, looking Hobbs directly in the eye.

'We've sort of grown tired of your company, reverend,' the sergeant replied with an evil grin.

'You're not really army men, are you?'

'The hell we're not,' advised Hobbs.

'Then why are you behaving in such a fashion?'

'We have our reasons, let's just leave it at that.'

'OK. So what now?'

'Yeah, what do you need with my boy and young Nancy?' asked Burrows.

'We're leavin',' advised Hobbs, 'and they're a sort of insurance to make sure you co-operate with us.'

'In God's name what sort of men are you?' responded Burrows, easing out of the arms of his tearful wife to take a full stride towards the soldiers.

'Back up, mister,' warned Hobbs with a deft flick of his gun. 'Another step and you'll be buzzard-meat.'

Fielding spoke calmly. 'Don't do anything foolish, Frank. Let's hear them out first.' The man backed up into the arms of his wife and stood silently glaring at the sergeant.

'Very wise, reverend,' remarked Hobbs. 'Now if you'll all just do as you're told, no one need get hurt.'

'What exactly do you want of us?' asked Fielding.

'First we want all your guns in a nice neat little pile right where you're standing,' he replied, pointing at the ground.

'I don't think we can agree to that,' said the reverend, 'not with those murdering Comanches so close at hand.'

'I don't care whether you agree or not, you'll do it just the same,' snapped the sergeant.

'What if we won't give up our guns?' asked Burrows, with a determined edge to his voice.

'Then you better start using them,' replied Hobbs. 'But if you do, your kid'll be the first to get it.'

'Do as he says,' said Fielding.

'Oh, and before you lay 'em down I want all the shells emptied out on the ground at your feet,' added Hobbs.

One by one the men, including a still deeply troubled Frank Burrows, emptied their guns and walked slowly forward to drop their weapons on the pile.

'Now, that's better,' said Hobbs. 'OK, now we need enough food to see us through the next few days and some civilian clothes. Send some of the women to fix us up,' he barked.

'I doubt we'll find anything to fit you, sergeant,' said Fielding with an air of disgust.

Hobbs patted his huge girth good-naturedly. 'You'll just have to do the best you can then, won't you,' he replied, not put out in the least. 'Maybe I might just manage to squeeze into something belonging to that big, crazy Irishman.'

The hairs on the back of Pete Forster's neck bristled with indignation, but he held his tongue. He caught the eye of his wife and indicated to her by an upward nod of his head that she should go and fetch some of his spare duds. Mary hurried off with some of the other women to collect the items demanded by the sergeant. They were back within a matter of minutes. Having laid the clothes and food down in front of the soldiers they rejoined their menfolk and waited anxiously to see what would happen next.

'Is that all you want?' asked Fielding.

Hobbs looked up from the pile of clothing and food before him with a satisfied smirk on his face. 'Hardly,' he replied, without changing his expression one iota.

'What else then?'

'Money.'

'Money!' exclaimed the reverend, with an incredulous look on his face. 'You're crazy. We're simple folk, we don't have any money, leastways none to speak of.'

'What do you take me for, reverend? No one travels halfway across the country to make a fresh start lessen they've got somethin' stashed away.'

'No one on this train has more than a few dollars to their name,' replied Fielding, his voice a curious mixture of resentment and sorrow. 'Carpet-baggers and Yankee taxes saw to that.'

'That being the case we'll just take what you

have,' replied Hobbs.

An angry murmur went up from the crowd. They were ordinary, decent folk, who had worked hard all their lives. The war, and its after-effects, had left them broken. Everything they had left in the world was contained in the wagons that had become their homes for two long months.

Fielding understood the burning anger and fierce resentment in his flock's heart, he shared it, but he knew that blood would inevitably be spilt if they didn't comply. Without a word he turned away from the belligerent, but helpless crowd, and walked slowly off towards his wagon. He returned with thirty freshly-minted gold Eagles which he handed over to the smirking sergeant without a word.

'Now that's what I call a good start,' said Hobbs as he pocketed the coins. 'So who's gonna be next?'

Slowly, one by one, the head of each family went to collect what money they had. The money was stashed in the renegades' waiting saddlebags. When they were full, Baker tied them in place behind their saddles while Hobbs continued to hold court. 'We're taking the kids with us just to make sure you don't follow.'

There was an audible gasp amongst the still crowd.

'You can't expect us to just stand idly by while you ride away with our kids,' stated Fielding.

'You don't have a choice,' replied the sergeant. With a sideways motion of his head he beckoned to his companions to get the kids and themselves mounted.

'Damn your black heart, sergeant,' yelled Pete

Forster, as Hobbs backed slowly towards his horse while Cooper kept his gun trained on the crowd. 'How can you risk the lives of our kids in such a callous fashion?'

Hobbs halted beside his horse and met the gaze of those at the front of the seething, frightened crowd with a confident air of stoic defiance. 'I can do anything I wish, seeing as how I hold all the aces. But don't worry, nothing's gonna happen to your kids, so long as you don't follow. We'll leave them at Morgan's Ford.'

'Where's that?' asked Fielding, knowing that further reasoning or argument was pointless.

'It's a small settlement about twenty miles west of here. They'll be quite safe there.'

'If you make it that far. The Comanches might have other ideas.'

'We'll make it. Those Comanch' are gonna be a mite more interested in what you folks have to offer them than in chasing after us.'

'If any harm comes to those kids I swear we'll hunt you down like dogs,' promised Frank Burrows with a look of pure hate on his face.

Without another word the soldiers and their young hostages turned their horses about and trotted off towards the edge of the compound. 'When we go, we go like bats out of hell,' said Hobbs to those who rode beside him. With that they spurred their horses on through the narrow gap between the wagons and sped off at top speed into the night.

The pilgrims surged forward in a reflex action to watch them vanish into the darkness. Everyone held their breath and listened to the receding beat of the horses' hooves. They all hoped, for the sake of the hostages, that the soldiers would manage to evade the Comanches. The minutes ticked by. No gunfire or terrifying warcries rose up to shatter the quiet that had descended over the camp. They knew then that the group had got away.

EIGHT

Kane had the posse up and mounted while the moon was still completing its journey through the night sky. They rode slowly westward in the wake of the wagon-train, ever alert for any sign of trouble. The vast, flat, wide-open, grassy country was such that it could have hidden a thousand armies. And somewhere, within striking distance, they all knew a Comanche war party was prowling the territory. It was a sobering thought.

Close to noon Kane suddenly pulled up short in front of his rapidly tiring companions. They drew their mounts to a halt alongside him, curious to know why he had stopped. Each of them scanned the gently undulating prairie with their keen eyes, trying to make out what had caught the scout's attention.

'The wagons are about a mile or so ahead of us,' he said in response to the puzzled faces that confronted him.

'How can you tell?' asked Halliday, keen to learn something that might be of use to him in the future.

'I can smell Comanch',' advised Kane casually. 'And that means the train can't be far away either.'

'What are you aiming to do?' asked York.

'We'll ride in easy and take a look,' replied Kane.

The prairie sloped deceptively upwards for the next half-mile. When they were about to top the crest of the long grassy incline, Kane bade them dismount. Leaving Halliday behind to watch the horses they went forward on all fours. At the top they cautiously peeked over the rim and gazed at the country below. Not fifty yards from where they lay with their stomachs flat to the ground, were a dozen mounted Comanches. All were naked to the waist and painted for war. Away to the left of the main group were six more. Their lean, muscular, bronzed bodies coated in oil and buffalo-grease fairly glistened in the mid-day sun. It was a sight to strike terror into the hearts of the bravest of men.

Directly ahead of the fearsome-looking Indians, a further quarter of a mile out on the flat prairie bottom, stood the wagons of the besieged train. Kane nodded in silent approval at the way the pilgrims had arranged their defences. The small tight circle provided them with good cover and an excellent field of fire. It appeared that someone knew what he was doing. Two of the wagons had lost their canvas tops to fire, several more showed distinctive scorch marks.

He silently motioned to the others to withdraw backwards down the incline. They regrouped by the horses. Kane kept his voice calm and low as he addressed his companions. 'There are enough of them to do a lot of damage. They'll keep hittin' 'em and gradually wear the pilgrims down.'

'What do you aim to do?' asked Brady.

'I figure to give those Comanch' somethin' of a surprise,' he replied.

'What do you have in mind?'

'If we raise enough dust and holler like banshees I'm pretty sure we can convince 'em that they have an entire regiment of cavalry bearing down on them.'

'But what happens when they find out they don't?' asked Phillips.

'I don't figure they'll hang around long enough to check our measure,' insisted Kane. 'A Comanche will chase a thing 'til he figures he's chased it enough and then he'll quit. Sometimes they'll quit when it appears that there ain't no good reason for them to. Our intervention should be sufficient to convince 'em that it's time to settle for what scalps they've got and head on home.'

'But what if you're wrong?'

'Then there'll be plenty of 'em to go round!' It was said with a grin, but it did little to inject any humour into the situation. The posse was scared, and rightly so. 'Pity we don't have a bugler,' remarked Kane casually as his eyes took one last sweep of the area.

'We do,' interjected Gannon smugly.

'You're a bugler?'

'Yeah.'

'You got it with you?'

'In my saddlebag.'

'Then let's go make music.'

Gannon went to his mount and fumbled about inside the saddlebag. He came up with a slightly battered and tarnished bugle that had definitely seen better days, which he held up proudly for all to see. 'Hope it plays better than it looks!'

exclaimed Phillips as they followed on behind Kane.

They rode for half a mile, back the way they had come, before Kane had them dismount by a small grove of trees. He asked them to spread out and search for large, firm branches that could be tied together to form a travois for each horse. He planned to have the group tie their saddle-blankets to the travois and drag them at speed behind their horses to raise a great cloud of dust. From a distance the disturbance, combined with the yelling and the sounding of the charge, would take on the appearance of a large group of horsemen riding to the aid of the threatened wagons.

Thirty minutes later they reformed in a crescent shape, fifteen yards apart, ready to mount their death-defying charge. 'Remember,' said Kane, 'if they ain't fooled we just ride right on through them. You won't have time to pick and choose your targets, so just blaze away and keep on going 'til you're inside the circle.' They all nodded, but no one said a word.

Each man seemed lost in his own thoughts. York, who always looked so calm and assured on the outside, had butterflies in his stomach. Halliday felt a chill run down his spine as he contemplated what lay ahead. He wiped a dirty hand across his sweaty brow and licked his lips nervously. Gannon's throat felt dry. He swallowed hard and then spat on the ground in order to make it possible for him to blow the charge when the time came. The two civilians looked anxiously at each other. Fighting Comanches was not an everyday occurrence for them. It was something they would much rather have left to the army.

They rode forward at a walk, guns at the ready, maintaining the wide crescent shape they had adopted. When they were a hundred yards from the enemy Kane ordered the charge. Gannon's bugle echoed through the hot, still afternoon air to inspire the horses to greater speed. They all roared at the top of their voices as they charged over the rim, causing a dust-storm to rise high in the air all about them.

They plunged down the slope constantly looking all about them for any sign of the enemy. But there wasn't a single Comanche to be seen. It was as if the country had simply swallowed them up. When they hit the flat bottom-land they noticed a great cloud of dust, similar to their own, several hundred yards beyond the wagons. Kane had been proved right, the Comanches had made themselves scarce. The posse didn't slow up until they were right on top of the astonished pilgrims inside the circle.

Kane rode in through a narrow gap between two of the wagons and reined in close to where the train's livestock were tethered. He swung down out of the saddle as the others drew up beside him.

'Who are you?' boomed an unfriendly voice at his elbow, as the scout dismounted.

He turned his head and locked eyes with a tall, shabbily-dressed, bearded man who was pointing a shotgun straight at him. Kane was taken aback by his hostility. 'This ain't exactly the sort of welcome I had anticipated,' stated Kane in a calm, unwavering voice. His eyes never left those of the man holding the shotgun.

'You ain't answered the question,' the man retorted. He took a step forward so that the barrel of the gun was no more than three feet from Kane's midriff.

The scout's eyes narrowed. 'Mister, I don't like having a shotgun pointed at my belly.' His face betrayed no emotion, but before the man knew what had happened Kane was on him. In the blinking of an eye the gun was pushed aside and the man was roughly deposited on the ground. Kane picked up the shotgun, snapped it open, withdrew the cartridges and threw it down next to the man at his feet. 'If you're gonna shoot someone, friend, don't waste time telling him what you aim to do, just go ahead and do it.'

More and more people were arriving on the scene with each passing second. There was an angry feel to the crowd. 'Who's in charge here?' demanded Kane, noticing that more guns were arriving on the scene.

'I am,' said Fielding, pushing his way through the pilgrims. 'Who are you?' he asked in a powerful, yet slightly nervous voice.

'It seems to me,' said Kane, 'that you could afford to be a mite more friendly towards us, considering we just drove off your unwelcome visitors.'

Fielding looked into his eyes and then gave an almost imperceptible nod. 'We are truly grateful for your timely intervention, but I'd still like to know who you are?'

'The name's Kane. I scout for the army.'

'And the others?'

'They're all members of a posse out of Miller Springs.'

'Three of your men are in uniform. Since when have cavalrymen ridden in a civilian posse?'

'The men we are after are soldiers.'

'What did they do?'

'They murdered a sheriff.'

His revelation caused an even greater murmur amongst the assembled crowd. The atmosphere changed from one of hate and suspicion to one of excited animation. 'The men you're chasing,' said Fielding, 'would one of them be a sergeant by the name of Hobbs?'

Kane nodded. 'They've been here?'

'Yes,' replied Fielding. He gave them a full account of everything that had happened. 'Maybe now you can understand why those blue uniforms weren't exactly a sight for sore eyes,' he concluded.

The scout gave a sheepish grin. 'Yeah,' he agreed.

'The question is, what do we do now?'

Kane pushed his hat back. 'It seems to me,' he said, 'that it would be best if I left the three troopers with you to see your party safely through to Morgan's Ford, while me and the two deputies ride on ahead to try and catch up with the hostages.'

'There's a few men on the train who I'm sure would like to go with you,' replied Fielding.

'It would be best if they remained with their families,' advised Kane. 'The chances are you won't see hide nor hair of any more Comanches, but there's no sense in taking chances. We'll get your kids back. You have my word on it.'

Fielding turned to face his flock. 'I think we have no choice but to trust these men.' Not a single voice was raised in argument. The reverend turned back to face the scout. He extended his hand and said, 'Get it done.'

Kane nodded. 'Just do as the trooper York tells you and you'll make out fine. We'll meet you at Morgan's Ford.'

NINE

Just before noon they dismounted beside one of the countless small streams that criss-crossed the empty, desolate wastes of northern Texas, and happily rested saddle-sore rumps and cramped muscles.

Baker was feeling decidedly unhappy with life. He knew he was in over his head. Things hadn't panned out the way he had expected. Sheer bravado and youthful arrogance had led him astray. Back at the fort he had always been subjected to a great deal of teasing and torment. All he had ever wanted to do was show them all that he was a man growed. That was why he had gone off with Hobbs and Cooper to drink in the saloon. Instead of proving his manhood he had got himself into a situation that had somehow snowballed totally out of control.

Nancy hadn't spoken a single word to him during their long ride. Every time he had ridden up beside her she had turned her head away and scorned his approaches. It bothered him, for he cared about her. In different circumstances he might even have set his cap for her.

After filling his dry canteen at the stream he decided to try one more time to get her to talk to him. He strode purposefully over to where she and Billy were sitting with their backs against a small tree. 'I thought you might like a cool drink,' he said, proffering the canteen.

She turned away with a haughty toss of her head and stared blankly out across the open prairie.

'She don't want no drink from you,' stated young Billy Burrows angrily.

'Please talk to me, Nancy?'

'Why don't you just leave her alone,' snarled Billy.

'And why don't you just shut your mouth, kid, before I take my belt to you,' shouted Hobbs from the other side of the narrow stream.

'Don't you dare lay a hand on him!' screeched Nancy, putting a protective arm around him.

'I'll give him the licking of his life if he don't get a grip of his sassy tongue. And the same goes for you too, my gal.'

Billy came to his feet with an angry scowl on his face. He had always been a spunky kid and despite the threat he was more than willing to let his feelings be known. But Nancy wasn't prepared to let the boy talk his way into a beating. 'Be quiet, Billy,' she said very calmly, as she moved to his side. 'I can look out for myself.' As the boy started to pout she swung round to catch the eye of Baker. 'Keep away from me, Daniel Baker, we have absolutely nothing to say to each other.'

'Nancy, please! You don't understand.'

'You're darned right about that. I don't understand what I ever saw in you!'

'I didn't want them to bring you along, honest.'

'Do you expect me to believe that?'

'Hobbs made me do it.'

'You're pathetic,' she snapped.

'Want to borrow my belt?' laughed Hobbs, wading across the stream towards the quarrelling couple. 'Seems to me you need to teach her a little respect. Or maybe you'd like me to do it for you?'

'No!' yelled Baker, placing himself between Nancy and the approaching sergeant. 'You won't touch her.'

'Getting kinda brave all of a sudden, aren't we, kid?' As the sergeant reached the bank, a few feet away from where the two of them were standing, Baker pulled and cocked his gun in one slick movement. Hobbs froze. An initial scowl immediately gave way to a broad grin. 'You ain't got the nerve to shoot me, boy.'

'Don't push me, Hobbs. I swear I'll do it if you try to hurt her.'

But his trembling gun-hand convinced Hobbs that he wouldn't fire. He advanced on him slowly, keeping his eyes firmly on the kid's gun.

'Plug him!' bellowed Billy, in high expectation of a bloody gunfight between his captors.

'Don't come any nearer,' advised Baker. He moved the gun slowly from side to side threateningly, but Hobbs kept coming. Baker's finger tightened on the trigger. He knew he had to shoot or risk being torn apart. Suddenly, his head felt as if it was about to explode and everything went completely black.

Hobbs would have lost his bet had it not been for Cooper's timely intervention. While all eyes were trained on Hobbs and Baker, he had strolled silently up behind the kid and hit him alongside the ear with the barrel of his gun.

'I do believe that little son-of-a-bitch would have shot me after all!' exclaimed a grinning Hobbs, standing over the boy soldier.

'Crazy kid,' said Cooper, shaking his head.

Hobbs looked down at Baker and gave his body a sharp kick in the ribs. 'So you were willing to kill me just to protect your little piece of baggage,' he drawled in menacing fashion. Then without a second thought he drew his gun and shot Baker in the back. The body jerked convulsively and then went limp. A red stain rapidly spread across the back of his shirt. Nancy screamed hysterically and threw her hands up over her face.

Cooper stepped forward and grabbed hold of Hobbs by his gun-arm. 'You didn't need to do that,' he stormed, hardly able to believe what had happened.

Hobbs tried to pull his arm away from the vice-like grip, but Cooper held on in determined fashion, partly because he feared that he himself might become a target for the sergeant's next bullet. 'The kid was weak,' growled Hobbs, looking the shocked Cooper straight in the eye. 'He was becoming a liability. Might have ended up getting us all hung.'

'You didn't need to kill him,' argued Cooper, letting go of his arm.

'You've gone soft, Cooper,' said Hobbs, putting up his gun.

Cooper tilted his dusty, weathered, discoloured hat and scratched his sweaty, matted hair. 'Maybe you're right,' he agreed with a slight nod of his head, 'but damn it to hell, sarge, he was still just a kid.'

Hobbs shrugged his massive shoulders. 'It's

done now. Let's get out of here.'

'We gonna bury Baker first?'

'Naw, let the buzzards have him,' he replied, looking down distastefully on the body. As Cooper set off towards the horses, the sergeant spoke sharply to Nancy and the wide-eyed, shocked little boy who clung to her side. 'You, girl, quit that wailing or I'll really give you something to fuss about. And you, boy, don't cause me any grief or you'll get what Baker got. Do ya hear me?'

The trembling youngster just nodded. Nancy pulled Billy closer to her. 'It's OK, Billy, we just got to do as he says until we reach the settlement, then everything's gonna be all right.' The frightened boy lifted his head towards her and nodded slowly. She gave his head a friendly rub and whispered into his ear, 'Don't fret now, I'll take care of you.'

Minutes later they rode off at a leisurely pace to the south-west. Only Nancy gave a backward glance towards the prostrate young soldier, who was still lying exactly where he had fallen. She regretted that her last words towards him had been spoken in anger. Despite his part in things she hadn't wanted to see him killed.

Within the hour the character of the land through which they were travelling underwent a dramatic transformation. Gone was the seemingly endless, flat, grassy plain and in its place was a land of gently rolling, broken hills. They continued westward through a broad, tree-lined valley.

It was as they left the valley and started to climb a long, low hill that Nancy's ears picked up a strange, distant drumming sound. The others heard it too. Hobbs instantly reined in.

'What is it?' asked Cooper from the rear.

Hobbs removed his hat and used the dusty sleeve of his army jacket to wipe away the perspiration from his brow. He stood up in the stirrups of his saddle and listened intently. 'Doggoned if I know,' he admitted. 'But the way the earth's quaking it feels as if all the armies of the world are on the march.' With that he spurred his mount forward at the trot towards the crest of the hill.

When they topped the rise their eyes beheld an awesome sight. There in the wide valley-bottom below, for as far as their eyes could see, was a thick, black, moving mass of huge shaggy beasts under a blanket of dust.

God!' exclaimed Hobbs. 'Did you ever see such a sight?'

'Buffalo,' said Cooper in an awed whisper.

The great herd continued their unhurried trek up the valley, totally oblivious to the party on the hill. On the far side of the valley a small pack of wolves were tracking the great hairy beasts, in the hope of picking off an unwary young calf or sick elder statesman. 'Quite somethin', ain't it?' stated Hobbs. 'Enough meat there to feed the whole United States Army for the next five years.'

Cooper, having got over his initial sense of wonder, took a more pragmatic view. 'I don't like it, sarge. Mark my words, where there's buffalo there'll also be Injuns thicker than fleas round a hog.'

Hobbs grinned and gave the back of his neck a cramp-easing rub. 'You worry too much,' he said. 'In point of fact them buffalo are gonna come in mighty useful.'

'How so?' queried Cooper with a frown.

'If we ride down nice and easy so as not to spook 'em, we'll be able to mingle with the herd for a while and cover our tracks.'

'But I thought you said no one from the train would be fool enough to follow us?'

'Why take a chance? An hour with our horned friends down there and no one will ever be able to pick up our trail.'

'Won't that take us out of our way?'

'Maybe a little, but that won't matter too much.'

Hobbs spurred his mount on down the slope towards the unbroken sea of animals. Billy and Nancy followed on in his wake with an anxious, still unconvinced Cooper bringing up the rear. One or two of the great beasts moved rapidly out of their way as they approached the outer perimeter of the herd, but once they were in amongst them the rest paid them no heed. Within a matter of minutes they were a part of the great, moving mass, hidden from view by the dust and the bulky animals themselves.

It was late in the afternoon when the three-man posse found the spot where the renegades had had their parting of the ways. On Kane's instruction Brady and Phillips watered their horses while the scout took a good look around. It didn't take him long to find the bloodstain in the flattened grass.

'You found something?' asked Phillips from the stream.

'You could say that,' replied Kane without looking up.

'What is it?'

'Seems like our friends had a falling out.'

Brady and Phillips moved to his side and looked

down at the patch of reddened grass. 'Looks like dried blood,' said Brady, removing his hat to scratch at his receding hairline.

'That's just what it is,' responded Kane. 'From the amount of blood he's lost the man ought to be dead.'

'So where's the body?' asked Phillips.

'The body got up and rode off,' quipped Kane.

'How long ago?'

'Not more than an hour, I'd say.'

'Then we're getting closer,' stated Brady with genuine enthusiasm.

'To one of them, at least,' agreed Kane good-naturedly. 'If he's hurt as bad as I think he is, we should catch up with him sooner rather than later.' They promptly returned to their horses and took up the chase.

Forty minutes later, as the sun neared the western horizon, they crossed the path of the great buffalo-herd. Kane was the only one amongst them who recognized the sign for what it was. 'What the hell caused this?' asked Brady, irritably slapping away a persistent mosquito. The biting insects were always at their most ferocious as evening approached.

'Buffalo,' replied Kane.

'Must have been a big herd,' offered Phillips.

'It was,' confirmed Kane.

'How are we ever gonna pick up their tracks in amongst all that trampled earth?' sighed Brady.

'We're not,' advised Kane. 'We don't need to look for sign anymore. We know where they're heading. All we got to do is get ourselves to Morgan's Ford.'

'You figure that big sergeant thinks he's safe from pursuit about now?'

'That's exactly what I figure,' agreed the scout.

'So let's go show him just how wrong a guy can be,' joked Brady, urging his horse on through a veritable curtain of buzzing insects.

Much to their surprise they picked up the trail of the lone, wounded rider on the far side of the wide, shallow valley. But as evening gave way to twilight and then ultimately to the inky-black cloak of night, it became increasingly difficult for Kane to follow the tracks. There was no moon to aid him in his task, for the sky had started to cloud over just before sunset. He eventually lost the trail altogether. Not that any of them were unduly worried, for as he had already pointed out, they knew where their quarry was heading anyway.

Had it not been for the unique understanding between Kane and his horse they would have ridden right past the wounded fugitive. As they made their way slowly westward across the darkened prairie the horse sensed the presence of another of his kind. His ears pricked up and he gave a low snort. Kane immediately reined in, knowing that his mount had detected something of interest beyond his range of vision.

'What is it?' whispered Brady as he stopped beside the scout.

'I don't know yet,' replied Kane, in an equally low voice. Then they all heard the telltale whinny of a horse somewhere nearby. In a flash Kane was out of the saddle and bounding away softly and surefooted – in the direction of the sound. Brady and Phillips drew their rifles and nudged their horses off in pursuit of the rapidly disappearing scout. Brady paused just long enough to pick up the trailing reins of Kane's mount.

Kane came upon the horse within a matter of seconds. It pawed the ground nervously at his silent approach. 'Easy, boy,' said the scout, reaching out a hand to pat it lightly on the neck. 'Now where's your rider?' He quickly circled about in search of the trooper, who he knew could not be far away. A low moan, followed by a painful cough, helped Kane to locate him.

He found him lying flat on his back with his head propped up on a low rock. The trooper made no attempt to defend himself. 'You must be Baker,' said the scout. The boy gave a raspy, pain-filled cough.

'Yes sir,' he replied softly.

'What happened?' Before the boy could answer Brady and Phillips arrived to stand behind the squatting scout.

'That's one of 'em,' snarled Phillips. He spat on the ground in contempt.

'Tell me what happened,' repeated Kane.

Baker looked scared to death. He swallowed hard and fought hard to suppress another bout of coughing. 'I ain't rightly sure, but I guess Hobbs shot me.'

'Why?' asked Brady.

'He was going to hurt Nancy and I tried to stop him.'

'The girl hostage?'

'Yes.'

'I don't believe a word of it.'

'It's the truth, mister, honest.' He was very weak. It had taken a great deal of effort to ride so far. Having to answer their questions was rapidly draining what little strength he had left.

'I don't figure there's any tree nearby,' said

Phillips. 'We'll just shoot the son-of-a-bitch instead.' He chambered a fresh round into the breach of his Winchester and pointed the rifle at the boy's head. Kane came to his feet quickly and grabbed hold of the barrel of the gun. 'What the hell, Kane,' stormed Phillips. 'Ain't it what we came for?'

'No it ain't,' corrected Kane. 'He's going back to Fort Walsh for trial, as agreed with Bates.'

'But he's a no-good, murdering little ass-hole,' interjected Brady.

'You ain't gonna do it and that's that,' insisted the scout defiantly.

'Haven't you ever felt the urge to kill a man?' argued Phillips.

The question touched a nerve deep in the scout's subconscious. Instantly his mind went back to a bitter day just prior to the war when he had stood by helpless as his mother had been gunned down outside her own house. Even after six long years the memory still frequently haunted his lonely nights out on the trail. Yes, he admitted to himself, there was a man he could gun down in cold blood without a second thought. But that was different.

'By the looks of him it's all rather academic anyway,' said Brady, looking down at the frightened, ghostly-white trooper. The cowboy's statement brought Kane out of his brief trance. 'He'll probably die before morning.' Phillips looked at his friend. 'Let it be,' advised Brady, putting a hand on his shoulder.

Phillips pulled away from his friend and waved a dismissive hand in the air. 'All right, have it your way, Kane,' he said.

While the two cowboys took care of making a litter for their captive, Kane began to interrogate him in the hope of gleaning some useful information. The net was rapidly closing on the renegades. By morning the chase would be over.

TEN

Hobbs and his party arrived at Morgan's Ford as twilight settled over the land. A dim light shone through the front window of the only major building at the isolated river crossing. The wooden-planked, leaky structure with its sod roof and loose panes of glass had a real weather-beaten look about it. They could make out two other buildings, a tiny, flimsy-looking outhouse at the front and a ramshackle barn-come-stable at the rear.

The trading-post had been hastily erected in the late 1850s, ostensibly to meet the needs of the growing band of small ranchers, dirt-farmers and buffalo-hunters who were arriving in the region in ever-increasing numbers. It was named after Bob Morgan, the shady, hard-drinking character who built it. He still lived there with his young Comanche squaw, Dancing Moon.

'Looks nice and quiet,' observed Hobbs.

'Sure does,' agreed Cooper.

'I hear tell Morgan ain't too particular about who he does business with, so it'll suit our purpose just fine,' stated Hobbs.

'What else do you know about him?'

'Not much. Just that he doesn't have too good a

reputation in these parts. A lot of people reckon he's well in with a bunch of Comancheros who operate from below the border.'

'You mean he helps run guns and whiskey to the Indians?'

'That's exactly what I mean.'

'Sounds like an interesting sort of fella. I can't wait to meet him.' Cooper gazed up towards the heavens in response to a faint, distant rumble of thunder. Dark clouds were billowing in from the north. The wind was getting up, but the air still felt heavy and oppressive. 'I hope you intend staying over 'til morning?' he said. 'I don't fancy being caught out in the rain.'

Hobbs glanced upwards into the gathering gloom. 'We ain't in any rush,' he replied.

'You reckon the trader's got any good liquor down there?' asked his companion expectantly.

'Good liquor, no. Gut-rotting moonshine, most certainly,' replied Hobbs.

'What about us?' cried Nancy above the wind.

'Oh, I have plans for you, little lady,' advised Hobbs, grinning evilly.

'You said you'd let us go once we reached Morgan's Ford,' she said, with a hint of anger and frustration in her voice.

'And I will, come morning.'

'Might be that this is as good a time as any to get into our civilian clothes,' suggested Cooper.

Hobbs nodded in agreement. 'No point in arousing any unnecessary curiosity.' They dismounted and changed quickly. Although nothing was an exact fit the clothing was comfortable enough. Once they were ready they boldly rode up to the front of the trading-post and then dismounted. 'When we get inside, you two kids keep your mouths shut, you hear?' warned Hobbs, as Cooper led the way towards the door. The two youngsters exchanged worried glances, then nodded.

When Cooper pushed against the door he found it barred from the inside. Hobbs stepped past the hostages and pushed his accomplice aside. he banged his fist aggressively and repeatedly on the door and yelled at the top of his voice to be let in.

A moment later they heard the sound of approaching footsteps. The door creaked open and a small, weasily-looking, middle-aged man came out gun in hand to look them over suspiciously. He had a dark, Latin type complexion, balding head and stubbly beard. His clothes were so dirty they almost looked as if they could have stood up on their own. He stank to high heaven of tobacco, cheap corn whisky and stale sweat.

'You want som'thin'?' he drawled through black, rotting teeth stained with tobacco-juice. It was his bad breath rather than the pistol that caused Hobbs to take half a step back in disgust.

'Are you Morgan?' he enquired, almost gagging on the unpleasant smell emanating from the man.

'Who wants to know?' came the reply.

'The name's Hobbs. Me and my friends need a few supplies and a dry roof over our heads 'til the storm blows over.'

'This ain't no hotel,' spat the man testily.

'We'll make it worth your while,' Hobbs assured him. For effect he jingled the gold coins in his pocket.

The pleasant sound immediately aroused the trader's interest. He smiled brightly and beckoned them inside. 'Come on in,' he said jovially. 'Maybe I can get ya a jug while we discuss your other needs.'

'That's mighty neighbourly of you, friend,' replied Hobbs. Their gallant host showed them to a bare, wooden table in a corner of the dimly-lit room.

The air smelt stale and musty. All manner of dry-goods, clothes and tools were displayed on low trestle-tables in the front part of the room and on tall racks against two of the walls. Two broad wooden planks supported by three upturned, empty flour-barrels formed a serving-counter. A huge pile of buffalo-hides and other pelts were piled up by the counter.

A young, brown-skinned woman suddenly materialized like a ghost out of the shadows carrying a one-gallon, ceramic liquor-jug. She set it down in the middle of the table. Hobbs eyed her approvingly. Her long, dark, braided hair, fine coppery skin and brown eyes created a very pretty picture which caused a stirring in his loins.

When she glided away across the bare earthen floor into the dark recess behind the counter he turned his attention to the jug on the table. He uncorked it and put it to his lips as Morgan came over to talk to him. 'Is it to your liking?' asked the trader.

Hobbs took a long gulp of the coarse, fiery liquid and then passed the jug over to the eagerly waiting Cooper. He spluttered once, caught his breath and said, 'Phew. What is that stuff? Horse liniment?'

Morgan laughed heartily. 'No, my friend, that is Mississippi's finest.'

'Highly debatable,' mused Hobbs, as Cooper nearly choked on the whiskey.

Their host laughed again, then addressed himself to the silent, brooding youngsters seated on the far side of the table. 'If you kids want something to drink it'll have to be water, I don't stock no sarsaparilla.'

'They don't want nothin',' snapped Hobbs, noticing the way Morgan was eyeing up Nancy. Although he was married, the trader wasn't averse to a piece on the side. However, the warning note in the big man's voice was enough to cool his ardour.

'How about something to eat?' demanded Cooper, sensing the tension between the two men.

'Beans and a little buffalo-jerky is as much as I can offer,' replied Morgan touchily. 'And it'll cost you a dollar a head.'

'That's robbery,' sneered Hobbs.

'A man has to make a living,' retorted Morgan firmly.

The empty growling in his stomach convinced Hobbs to pay up. 'All right, bring us four plates,' he ordered with a dismissive wave of his hand.

Just before Morgan returned with the food Hobbs sent Cooper out to put the horses in the barn. By the time he returned Hobbs and the youngsters had all but cleared their plates. His own food was barely lukewarm and anything but appealing. But he still ate as if it was a piece of prime steak.

Dancing Moon reappeared at the end of the meal to clear away the plates and replace the empty jug. As she turned to go, her hands full of dirty crockery, Hobbs reached out an arm and wrapped it tightly about her middle. 'You're as good a looking squaw as I've ever seen,' he announced in a loud, uncouth voice. The woman gave him a timid smile and tried to pull away. 'Where are ya going?' he asked. 'Stay a while and keep me company?'

'Unhand my woman,' demanded Morgan, coming forward from behind the counter. 'She ain't included in the price.'

Hobbs merely smiled and held on to Dancing Moon's waist. 'Maybe we could renegotiate then?'

'She's my wife, not some common whore you're used to picking up in saloons,' growled the angry trader as he reached the table. Before Hobbs knew what was happening Morgan had a sharply-honed, long-bladed Bowie knife at his neck. 'Let her go,' he said in a voice that clearly showed he meant business.

'OK, OK,' replied Hobbs, releasing her. 'I was only having a little fun.'

Morgan waited a few seconds and then slowly withdrew the knife. 'I've half a mind to turn you out now,' he said, spitting on the floor.

'Don't mind Hobbs any,' intervened Cooper, not relishing the prospect of a long, wet ride. 'He don't mean no harm.'

Morgan scowled. 'Keep away from my woman,' he barked before striding away.

'Better take it easy,' whispered Cooper. 'We can't afford no more trouble.' Hobbs merely scowled at him and then returned to the jug.

As the night wore on the two soldiers consumed a considerable amount of liquor. Nancy, appreciating the effect the drink was likely to have on them, decided to remove Billy and herself from the table. She rose slowly from her chair and took hold of Billy by the arm. Hobbs turned his glazed eyes towards her. 'Where do ya think you're going?' he demanded in a slurred voice.

'We're tired,' she replied. 'We're going to lie down in the corner and get some sleep.'

'All right,' he agreed with a hiccup. 'But stay away from the door.'

Nancy nodded. The youngsters then settled themselves in the corner of the room, facing the soldiers. To the girl's surprise Dancing Moon appeared a couple of minutes later with blankets to make the youngsters more comfortable. 'Thank you,' she said, as Dancing Moon smiled and moved away.

The troopers went on drinking late into the night. Some time after midnight Cooper finally collapsed into a drunken stupor. He lay sprawled across the table with his head resting on his elbows. A moment later Hobbs staggered outside to relieve himself. He left the front door swinging open in the wind behind him.

Nancy had been waiting patiently for just such a moment. She nudged Billy awake with her elbow, instantly putting a hand across his mouth to stifle his surprised cry. After checking that Cooper was still asleep she whispered into Billy's ear, 'Now's your chance to get out of here.'

The boy flashed her a frightened glance. 'No,' he replied. 'Hobbs will kill me.'

'Not if you go now,' insisted Nancy. 'He's just gone outside to pee. Go now while he's preoccupied.'

'What if he sees me?'

'He won't.'

'But he'll come after me when he sees I'm missing.'

'He'll never find you in the dark.'

'What about you?'

'I'll be fine.'

'You won't. He'll give you a whipping for sure. He'll know you put me up to it.'

'Billy, quit arguing and get out of here now before I give you a licking myself.'

The boy looked nervously towards the door and then at Nancy. 'I'll get help,' he said, finally giving in to her gentle urging.

She smiled reassuringly. 'Just go. Be light on your feet so he don't hear you,' she warned.

Billy pushed himself up the wall and tiptoed to the open door. When he hesitated Nancy feared he had lost his nerve. She was about to go to him when he suddenly took the bull by the horns and disappeared outside.

Billy turned left and hugged the wall. He paused, lost in the shadows of the building, a thin film of sweat on his brow, and tried to locate the sergeant. Almost immediately he heard the outhouse door bang shut. There came a loud cough followed by faltering, shuffling footsteps. He considered taking to his heels in the hope of outrunning the man. But fear and indecision numbed his muscles. He froze, closed his eyes, held his breath and prayed that he wouldn't be noticed. As the footsteps came closer he forced himself to open his eyes. As he did so the huge shape of the sergeant loomed up at him out of the darkness.

Hobbs never even looked in Billy's direction as he disappeared inside, kicking the door closed behind him. The boy sighed with relief and then took to his heels. He didn't slow down until he had covered a good quarter of a mile. After a quick backward glance to see if he was being pursued he jogged a further half-mile before pausing to rest.

He had been resting in the damp grass for just a couple of minutes when the clear, sharp report of gunfire echoing through the night air brought him to his feet. His first thought was that Hobbs had shot Nancy. For a moment he considered going back. But then he saw sense. Going back would only put his own life in danger. It was far better to make a run for it in the hope of finding help. He set off at a flat-out run, knowing that the dark was his only ally.

Nancy pretended to be asleep when Hobbs returned. He weaved unsteadily towards the table and slumped down in his chair. The inebriated, snoring Cooper never stirred. Hobbs reached inside his jacket, pulled out his tobacco-pouch and rolled himself a smoke. As he prepared to light up his eyes fell on the girl. 'My, if you ain't a pretty little thing,' he said softly. He rose up and swayed towards her.

Nancy heard him coming. She opened her eyes and pressed herself back against the wall. Knowing what he had in mind, her heart began to beat rapidly. 'Go away,' she pleaded, as he towered over her with an evil smirk on his stubbled face. His smile vanished in a trice when he noticed that the boy was missing.

'Where is he?' he demanded angrily, sweeping the room with his eyes. When she made no reply he bent forward and grabbed hold of the front of her dress. He pulled her roughly to her feet and slapped her hard across the face with the back of his hand. 'I said, where's the boy?'

'I don't know,' she lied. Tears began to well up in her eyes and a big red mark appeared on her cheek. He slapped her again even harder. She cried out in pain and fear.

'I ain't gonna ask you again.'

'Billy ran off while you were outside,' she said tearfully.

'And I'll bet you put him up to it,' he slurred, flinging her savagely back against the wall. She bounced off the wooden panels and slid slowly down to the floor. Hobbs staggered outside. 'Where the hell are ya hiding, boy?' he yelled at the top of his lungs. He turned a full circle in his vain attempt to locate the boy. In anger and frustration he drew his gun, fanned back the hammer and began firing wildly all about him.

'What in tarnation's all the shooting about?' demanded Morgan, as he appeared in the doorway dressed only in his long johns.

'Mind yer own business,' replied Hobbs. He fired another aimless shot into the dark.

'Have you gone plumb loco?' screamed the trader, stepping forward.

'Keep away from me,' warned Hobbs, turning to face him.

'Put that gun away.'

'Damn you,' said Hobbs. Without a second thought he brought his gun up and shot him twice in the chest. The force of the bullets caused Morgan to stagger back a pace. He looked down incredulously at the blood spurting from his chest. Slowly he sank to his knees, before toppling forward onto his face.

Hobbs calmly strolled forward and looked down at the trader. His countenance in death seemed to reflect both shock and outrage, as if he couldn't comprehend how or why it had happened. A woman's shrill, high-pitched scream caused Hobbs to look up. Morgan's squaw was standing in the doorway, a trembling hand over her mouth. Her first instinct was to run to her fallen husband, but as Hobbs advanced towards her she turned on her heels and bolted back inside the building.

Dancing Moon slammed the door shut behind her. Before she could bar the door, Hobbs shouldered his way inside. The force of his entry knocked her to the ground. He stood over her with a diabolical grin on his face.

'Whatssss, goooing on?' slurred Cooper, who had been awoken by the commotion. He raised his spinning, aching head from the table to gaze through red-rimmed, foggy eyes at the scene that was unfolding within the room.

'Keep out of it,' growled Hobbs.

Cooper made a valiant attempt to rise up out of his chair, but his head and body were not functioning in unison. With a loud, resigned sigh he slumped back down and closed his eyes.

'Well now, it seems to be your lucky night,' chuckled Hobbs, looking gleefully at the trembling Indian girl at his feet. 'You get to have me after all.'

She emitted a weak little cry and tried to slide away from him. 'No,' she screamed, as he reached down and grabbed hold of her long, braided hair. He yanked her roughly to her feet and pulled her into a passionate embrace. She kicked and fought like a wildcat, but he was just too big and powerful for her. 'Please, let me go,' she pleaded.

'Not on your life, little sister,' he replied, lowering his head towards her ruby-red lips. He had her backed up against the wall, so there was nowhere for her to go. When he finally withdrew his mouth she tilted her head forward and bit him tigerishly on the hand. Then she raked her long fingernails down the side of his obese face. Hobbs put a hand to his mauled face and let out a devilish roar of pain and rage. 'You bitch!' he bellowed, smashing his fist into the point of her jaw. She fell limply to the floor, hitting her head against the wall on the way down. With a painful moan she lapsed into unconsciousness.

Nancy's startled cry momentarily distracted him from the squaw. 'I'd almost forgotten about you, little girl,' he said. He knelt down and tore away the bright-red, silk sash that Dancing Moon had tied around the middle of her blue calico dress. He got up and walked over to where Nancy sat hunched up and terrified next to one of the large shelves which adorned the outer edges of the room.

Hobbs pulled her up and bound her wrists with the sash. He then found a thin leather belt on one of the shelves and used it to hobble her ankles. 'I don't think you'll be going anywhere,' he snarled as he turned and walked back to Dancing Moon.

She stirred a little as he bent down and lifted her into his arms. She was too weak to resist him as he carried her off to the small, curtained off-room at the back of the building. Her senses were slowly returning by the time he dropped her onto the bed. She stared up at him through wide, terrified eyes as he unbuckled his belt and removed his pants. When he fell on top of her and began to tear at her clothing like a demented animal she shut her eyes and let out a timid little cry. She tried to close her mind to the nightmare that was engulfing her. There was nothing she could do to save herself from the evil depravity of the beast, so she reasoned that the best thing to do was to submit meekly to his foul assault and get it over with as quickly as possible. The very last thing she remembered, before she mercifully passed out, was his hot, fetid breath upon her cheek and the awful, jackal-like laugh as he began to have his wicked way with her.

A screen of perspiration formed on Nancy's brow as she fought to loosen her bonds. The more she struggled the more they bit into her exposed flesh. In the end she gave up, gasping for breath, and lay still. At seventeen she was anything but wide-eyed and innocent. She knew exactly what was happening in the small back-room. Her greatest fear was that she would be next.

When Hobbs reappeared she gave a startled whimper. Cooper was snoring loudly at the table, dead to the world. The sergeant just grinned contentedly while Nancy cringed by the wall. 'You're next, little lady. I'm still man enough to handle two women in one night,' he said boastfully.

His desire to have the girl was overwhelming. It was his timely discovery of a fresh supply of liquor that saved her form his lusty attentions. His eyes fell on a dusty bottle of best Kentucky bourbon on the shelf behind the counter. He moved eagerly towards it, uncorked the bottle with his teeth and took a long swig of the warming liquor. He wiped a dribble from the corner of his mouth and then took a second swallow. 'Hey, wake up, Cooper, and try some of this,' he said. When his friend made no reply he edged his way slowly around the bar towards him. Halfway across the floor his legs gave out on him. He crashed to the floor, smashing the bottle on the way down. 'Too bad,' he said, gazing forlornly at the whiskey which was soaking into the floor. He closed his eyes and fell asleep where he lay.

Apart from Cooper's snoring a peaceful hush descended over the room. As the minutes ticked by and Hobbs showed no signs of stirring, Nancy began to relax. The man's drinking binge had provided her with a priceless commodity, time. Time for her to work on her bonds. Time for young Billy to find help. While the two soldiers slept on she wriggled her feet and went to work on the silk sash with her teeth with renewed vigour.

ELEVEN

Young Billy had long since lost all track of time. He had no idea how long he had been walking or where he was going. Not that he cared, for his only concern was to put as many miles as possible between himself and those back at the trading-post.

With no moon or stars to light the way he struggled on through the dark like a blind man. The odd rumble of distant thunder and flash of lightning caused him some anxiety, but in the event the storm passed way to the south of him. He did get wet from a rather heavy tail-end shower, but it was over almost as quickly as it had begun.

Every now and again he rested his tired legs and listened to the night. He was very scared. The scuttling of a disturbed rabbit, the call of a night-bird, the distant howl of a coyote, every little sound preyed on his mind and had him jumping at his own shadow.

With the first grey light of dawn showing in the eastern sky he came close to disaster. He was so tuckered out that he almost stepped on a coiled rattler. Fortunately for him the angry snake rattled its warning in the nick of time. Not daring to move in any direction he simply froze to the spot and watched mesmerized as the reptile's head swayed slowly from side to side. A cold bead of sweat formed on his brow. Finally, after what seemed like an eternity, the snake relaxed and slipped slowly away through the grass.

Unnerved by his close call Billy started to run blindly, at top speed, across the prairie. It proved to be his biggest mistake of the long night. He had gone less than half a mile when his right foot caught in an old, abandoned prairie-dog burrow. His ankle gave way and he crashed to the ground, crying out in pain and shock. Within seconds his ankle was swollen and badly discoloured. He lay on the damp ground clutching it in both hands.

After a couple of minutes he tried to stand up, but the very second his foot touched the ground it gave way beneath him and he fell back down. The pain was so intense that he began to sob. It was then that he heard the distant, rhythmic pounding of horses' hooves.

His heart started to beat with excitement. Aid was at hand. He yelled out, 'Help, over here!' at the top of his voice. Only then did it strike him that the riders could as easily be Comanches as a rescue-party. He heard the horses slow up. Almost immediately they changed direction and came on towards him at a steady lope. He held his breath. His whole body grew tense as the riders approached.

'It's a boy,' cried a surprised voice.

Billy relaxed. At least they weren't Indians out for his scalp. One of the men was soon at his side. 'Are you Billy?' he asked, going down on one knee beside him. The other men dismounted and came over to stand behind him.

'Yes sir,' he replied, wiping a tear from his cheek. 'Who are you?'

'Sam Kane. I'm an army scout. We ran into your folks a while back and when we found out what had happened we came after you.'

'I sure need your help,' Billy confessed, flexing his injured limb and grimacing in pain.

'Are you hurt?' asked Kane.

'Yeah. I twisted my ankle in a prairie-dog hole.'

'Is it broke?'

'I ain't sure.'

Kane took hold of Billy's leg at the knee and gently straightened it out. 'Quit squawking, kid, it don't look broke to me,' advised Phillips confidently.

'I reckon you wouldn't be so brave if it was your leg,' replied Billy sassily. They all laughed.

Kane carefully untied the boy's boot. As soon as he touched the ankle Billy cried out in pain. 'Easy, son,' he said in a low, calm, reassuring voice. Billy gritted his teeth. 'You got a bad sprain, but no broken bones. I'll bind it up for you. That'll make it a little easier for travelling on,' said Kane when he had finished his examination.

'Thanks,' said Billy.

The scout walked over to his horse and retrieved an old cotton shirt from his saddlebags. He tore it into long strips and then used it to bind Billy's ankle. When he had finished he questioned the boy at length about everything that had happened to him. The kid was only too willing to talk. As a result Kane gleaned a lot of useful information from him about what to expect at the trading-post.

'What are you aiming to do?' asked Brady at the end of their talk.

'Try and catch our friends with their pants down,' replied the scout.

'What about the boy?' interjected Phillips. 'We can't just leave him behind.'

'He'll go with us. He can ride double behind one of you.'

'Why can't he ride with you?' demanded Brady.

'Because I can't stand kids!' exclaimed Kane with a wry smile. Kane bent down, took the boy in his powerful arms and carried him over to the horses. They were almost there when Billy suddenly tightened his grip on the scout's neck. 'What's up?' he queried.

'Ain't he dead?' asked Billy nervously, pointing at the soldier in the travois right in front of him. 'I saw Hobbs shoot him.'

'Take it easy, son, he ain't gonna hurt you,' Kane assured him.

Billy relaxed his grip slightly. 'Just keep him away from me.'

'I will,' promised Kane.

It was the sound of the rain falling steadily from a dark, dreary, leaden dawn sky that caused Nancy to stir from her light sleep. The wind whipped the rain against the trading-post, rattling the loose panes of glass in the window-frames. On the ground outside, Bob Morgan lay where he had fallen.

Inside the still darkened room Nancy lay silent and passive with her back up against the wall listening to the melodic pitter-pattering of the rain on the roof above her head. Her eyes felt heavy and her body cold, weary and cramped. She had had only an hour's sleep at best, having struggled fruitlessly with her bonds throughout the hours of darkness.

A short while after Hobbs had collapsed on the floor she had tried to enlist the help of Dancing Moon. She had called out softly, trying to attract the Indian girl's attention. But when, after several attempts, no answer came, she had given up, fearing that Dancing Moon had met a similar fate to that of her unfortunate husband.

Her mouth felt dry and sore from all the biting and chawing at the silk sash about her wrists. At that moment she would have given anything for a cup of water. The room was still quite dark, for the kerosene lamp had long since gone out of its own accord and the first grey light of dawn was taking its time to penetrate through the two small windows at the front. She heard the rustling of a tiny mouse as it scurried about the floor somewhere on the other side of the room. It was all but drowned out by the rasping, unpleasant snoring of her two captors.

Although she felt very tired she fought hard to keep her eyes open. She didn't want to fall asleep again, not with the vile Hobbs so close at hand. There was no doubt in her mind that her torment would begin anew the moment he was awake. If she was to endure such unspeakable horrors then she wanted to see it coming rather than have it sneak up on her while she slept.

Shortly after dawn Hobbs woke up. He gingerly lifted himself up onto his elbows and gazed about the room through gaunt, rufescent eyes. His head throbbed so much it felt as if someone was using it as a drum. He raised a weary hand to the back of his stiff, tight neck and tried to massage some feeling back into it.

Nancy watched his every move through quick, darting, nervous eyes. When he finally came to his feet in lumbering, ungainly fashion, she tried to press herself even further back into the wall, as if in so doing she would become invisible. Hobbs paid her no mind. He was in no fit state to indulge himself in any carnal pleasures or violent actions. His physical exertions and drinking of the night before had left him feeling terribly drained and thoroughly out of sorts.

At the sound of Cooper's continued snoring he crossed the floor and gave him a hefty shove on the shoulder. He came round with a startled grunt. 'What's up?' he asked, lifting his head to peer at Hobbs through squinting, red-rimmed eyes.

'We got to be moving soon,' replied Hobbs.

'Aw, let me sleep some more,' Cooper grumbled. With that he rocked forward onto the front two legs of his chair, put his head down on his extended arms and closed his eyes. Summoning up what little energy he possessed, Hobbs kicked the chair out from under him. Cooper ended up in an ungainly heap on the floor. He climbed slowly back to his feet with an angry expression on his face. 'What'd ya do that for?'

'To get you moving,' Hobbs replied without apology. 'Now stay awake while I get us something to eat.' He strode away towards the curtained-off room behind the counter. 'Get out of bed, you lazy bitch, and fix us some breakfast,' he yelled as he approached the doorway. He pulled back the curtain and glared at the frightened figure of Dancing Moon. She was sitting up in bed with the single cotton blanket pulled up tightly to her neck. 'We're hungry, you Godless savage,' he growled. 'Move your ass and be quick about it.' She gave him a simple nod. He turned his back on her and returned to the main room.

Nancy watched and listened with quiet but vested interest. The revelation that Dancing Moon was still alive meant she no longer felt so alone and helpless. The two men continued to ignore her while they hungrily tucked into the cold biscuits and hot coffee that Dancing Moon served up for breakfast. By the time they finished they were more alert and in control of their faculties. 'More coffee,' growled Hobbs as he set his empty cup on the table in front of him.

Dancing Moon armed herself with a towel before she lifted the steaming hot coffee-pot off the stove and advanced towards the table to obey the sharp command. She never even glanced at either of the men seated at the table as she poured out the coffee. Having filled their cups she retreated quickly back to the stove.

Had either of the two soldiers turned to face her at that moment they would have seen the look of pure hate that burned in her eyes. It left a bitter taste in her mouth to think of the man who had defiled her riding away unpunished. What she wouldn't have given for a knife. Despite the inherent risks involved in tackling two armed men with just a knife, she would have welcomed the opportunity. Better to have died trying to avenge herself and her late husband than to have sat idly by while they escaped. But she had no such weapon. Then she suddenly remembered her dead husband's Bowie knife. It had to be somewhere in the bedroom. A brief smile touched her lips. She resolved then and there to search it out and put it to good use if the opportunity presented itself.

She didn't have long to wait. Right after breakfast Hobbs barked out an order. 'Go saddle our mounts,' he said, nudging the reluctant Cooper with his elbow.

'What's the rush?' asked his companion, who fancied a third cup of coffee before contemplating any kind of work.

'Just do as you're told,' growled Hobbs. 'And be quick about it.'

Cooper mumbled something unintelligible, kicked back his chair and stormed out of the room. Dancing Moon casually collected the dirty dishes from the table and carried them off to the sink in the back room. Once she was out of sight she wasted no time in searching out the Bowie knife. A smile came to her face when she found it on the floor beside the bed, amongst her dead husband's discarded clothing.

The posse reached Morgan's Ford not long after dawn. When they surveyed the tiny settlement they immediately spotted the body lying in front of the main building. 'You think they're still down there?' enquired Brady.

'I'd say so,' replied Kane.

'How do you want to play it?' asked Phillips. His general demeanour betrayed a desire for positive action.

'I don't want to rush in blind,' advised the scout. 'That could get the girl hurt.' His companions nodded. 'Brady, get yourself round to the far side of the barn at the rear and just sit tight 'til you get some sort of signal from me.'

'What if they come out?' he asked anxiously.

'Just stay put and wait.'

'OK.'

Despite his apparent agreement, Kane was less than convinced that Brady was going to play it his way. That was why he added, 'Don't do anything foolish,' as the cowboy slipped away.

'What do we do?' asked Phillips as they watched Brady race stealthily into position.

'We'll stake out the front of the building and just wait and see what happens,' advised Kane. As they made ready to move off he turned to speak to young Billy. 'Stay with Baker. We'll come for you when it's all over.' The boy looked set to argue, but at the last moment he thought better of it. He slunk away sulkily and took up station next to Baker.

Cooper turned his shirt collar up and pulled his hat down firmly on to his head as he stepped out into the gloomy morning air. He paused just long enough to take a quick look around before making a dash for the barn.

The horses snorted and moved about restlessly when he entered. 'Easy now,' he said softly, in an attempt to quieten them down. The unpleasant smell of sweaty animals, horse-dung and stale hay inside the dark, claustrophobic interior of the building was almost overpowering. It made him work quickly. In no time at all he had two of the horses saddled and ready to ride.

When he emerged from the murky depths of the barn he came face to face with a tall, silent figure dressed in a brown slicker. But it was the sight of the Winchester rifle pointed directly at him that halted Cooper dead in his tracks. 'Who the hell are you? What do you want?' he asked anxiously.

Brady ignored the rain that was dripping from the brim of his hat and kept his eyes firmly fixed on the soldier. 'Who I am don't matter,' he said casually. 'But as for what I want, well that should be obvious. I want you!'

A tingle of fear ran down Cooper's spine. The man had him dead to rights. Even so, being taken alive was not a prospect which appealed to him. Far better to make a try for his gun. He instinctively started to flex his fingers.

Brady read the warning sign correctly. 'Don't do it,' he advised, sensing that the advice would fall on deaf ears. Instantly Cooper dived to his right and grabbed for his gun. His bold, desperate gamble was doomed to failure. Two shots rang out from the rifle to slam into his chest before he was halfway to the ground. The reports echoed loudly out across the river. The horses Cooper had brought out of the barn reared up in fear and then galloped away.

Cooper lay sprawled on his back, unable to move. His breathing was shallow and laboured. Blood flowed freely from two holes in his upper torso and also from the corner of his mouth. Brady walked forward and stood over the dying soldier, cursing under his breath. Kane was going to be furious with him for not obeying orders. 'Better this way than at the end of a rope,' croaked Cooper, in a voice hardly above that of a whisper. Brady just nodded. The renegade's eyes closed and his head lolled limply away to the side.

The unexpected sound of gunfire instantly brought Hobbs to his feet. He dashed to the front window and peered anxiously outside. Two men were slowly approaching. The taller of the two carried a Winchester while the other had a double-gauge shotgun. 'Hell!' he exclaimed, banging his fist against the wall of the building.

Dancing Moon was only a couple of paces from Hobbs when the soft shuffling of her feet on the earthen floor betrayed her presence. He turned around in the nick of time. Another second and she would have plunged the upraised knife into the middle of his back. As she threw herself towards him he caught hold of her knife hand. His savage, twisting grip forced her to drop the weapon. He took hold of the neck of her dress and struck her a vicious blow to the side of the head. It sent her spinning away across the room. She crashed into the table and blacked out as she hit the floor.

Hobbs returned to the window. He frantically sought a way out of his predicament. The two men were drawing closer by the second. He knew the gunshots from the rear could only mean that Cooper was either captured or dead. A similar fate was bound to befall him too, if he didn't keep a cool head. They had him surrounded. There was no way he could make a break for his horse without getting shot down. But he did have one trump card left to play.

He strode purposefully over to Nancy, untied

her legs and yanked her to her feet. 'What are you going to do?' asked the terrified girl.

'Shut up and keep quiet,' he snapped. Nancy was powerless to resist Hobbs as he pushed her towards the door. Once outside he used her as a shield. 'That's close enough,' he yelled at the men closing in on the trading-post.

Kane and Phillips halted, but kept their firearms levelled on the doorway. 'Take it easy,' advised Kane. 'It's his move. Let's see what he does.' As he spoke he took in Brady's timely arrival on the scene. He quickly averted his eyes so as not to alert Hobbs to the presence of the cowboy skulking round the corner of the building. 'Why don't you come on out so we can discuss the situation?' suggested Kane. 'You can't hope to get away. We've too many guns.' He hoped to encourage the soldier out just far enough for the unseen cowboy to draw a bead on him. But Hobbs was far too wily a character to expose himself in so rash a fashion.

'I know you. Kane, ain't it?' The scout just nodded. 'Where are the others?' he growled, when his darting eyes failed to pick out any more opposition.

'They're around,' Kane assured him.

Hobbs spat on the ground and glared angrily at the two men standing before him. 'Call them out,' he instructed.

Kane played for time. After a brief hesitation he turned his head and yelled at the top of his voice for Billy to ride in. A couple of minutes elapsed before the boy appeared in sight. He came on at a fast lick, pulling the travois behind him. When he came level with Kane and Phillips he reined in.

Hobbs was clearly surprised to see the boy again. He was even more surprised to see Baker totter out of the travois to lean against the hindquarters of the horse. 'God-damn, Baker, you sure do take a hell of a lot of killing,' he sneered, shaking his head in disbelief. He was so taken aback by Baker's unexpected appearance that he forgot all about the unaccounted foe who had taken care of Cooper.

'Looks like we got somethin' of a stand-off,' said Kane.

'Hardly,' replied Hobbs contemptuously. 'If you want the girl to live you'll get out of my way.' Just for effect he proceeded to dig the barrel of his gun into her back. She squealed, more in surprise than pain. 'Lay your guns down and back off a ways,' he ordered.

'Do as he says,' replied Kane, dropping his rifle. Phillips reluctantly let go of his shotgun.

'The gunbelts too,' demanded Hobbs. Kane and Phillips exchanged glances then duly obliged. 'That's more like it,' grinned Hobbs, pushing his hostage forward a couple of paces.

Brady had been waiting patiently for just such an opportunity. The moment Hobbs came into his line of vision he stepped out from around the corner of the building and brought his rifle to bear on the soldier. Sheer bad luck cost him the element of surprise. A strong gust of wind caused his slicker to billow up in his face. It prevented him from firing and allowed Hobbs to react to his sudden appearance. The sergeant turned and fired twice from the hip. Brady dropped his rifle and slumped to the ground.

Hobbs spun back to face the men at his front.

The first thing he saw was Baker reaching for the rifle in the saddleboot by his shoulder. Before he could get it clear Hobbs shot him through the heart. Nancy screamed. She tore herself loose from the iron tight grip on her arm and ran to Baker's side. 'Daniel, oh Daniel,' she cried, kneeling down beside him. Billy eased himself carefully out of the saddle and hobbled over to join Nancy.

A smirking Hobbs took a couple of paces forward. 'Now it's time to settle up with you two,' he said, cocking the hammer of his gun. 'You first, Kane. Any last words?'

For many a long year Kane had lived his life on the very edge. He had always suspected that it might end in such a fashion. His one hope had always been that he would be able to go out with a gun or knife in his hand, mocking death to the very last. Now he knew that was not to be the way of it. But he was determined to face up to death with courage and dignity. There was no way scum like Hobbs was going to have the satisfaction of seeing him beg for his life like a dog. 'Go to hell, Hobbs,' he snarled contemptuously.

'You first, Kane.' mocked Hobbs, taking careful aim at the scout's head. As his finger tightened on the trigger a strange, enquiring look came over his face. He raised his eyebrows upwards and looked at Kane through incredulous, glazed eyes before toppling forward onto his face in the dirt.

Dancing Moon stood motionless in the open doorway. Up until that moment the huge girth of the sergeant had masked her from everyone's view. The Bowie knife she had sent whirling through the air to snuff out his evil life was still quivering in the middle of his back. The force she had generated to send it on its deadly way belied her tiny frame. 'I had a right to kill him,' she said, just before she broke down sobbing. Kane walked forward and touched her lightly on the shoulder. 'It was my right,' she repeated.

Kane nodded. 'You had the right,' he agreed.

Billy untied Nancy's hands. She went over and relieved Kane of Dancing Moon. The two women disappeared inside the trading-post with Billy hot on their heels. They left behind the acrid smell of spent cartridges and the stench of death.

'So it's finally over then,' remarked Phillips sadly, as he and Kane viewed the lifeless body of Brady.

The scout nodded. 'Let's bury the dead.'

TWELVE

The wagon-train rolled into Morgan's Ford late in the afternoon. There was much back-slapping and vigorous hand-shaking to go with the tearful reunions. When things had settled down a little Kane briefed Fielding on the release of the youngsters. He then suggested that the wagon-train should spend the night at the trading-post. Fielding readily agreed.

Although they still had far to go and many fresh dangers to face on the way to their promised land, a happy mood and an air of optimism prevailed amongst the pilgrims. Kane was very impressed by their attitude, courage and determination. As a result he changed his own plans. Rather than return to Miller Springs with Phillips he offered to escort the wagons to the New Mexican border.

When the wagons pulled out the next morning Kane was at their head. the three troopers saw him off before turning their mounts to the north for the long ride back to Fort Walsh.

Kane rode with the train as far as the town of Coyote Wells. There he managed to find a seasoned guide to take the pilgrims on to their final destination. After a few well-chosen words of advice to the reverend he said his goodbyes and set off back towards his native range.

Three weeks after the shoot-out at Morgan's Ford Kane rode back into the open compound at Fort Walsh. His journey had been long, hot, dusty, but not without interest. He had picked up some useful snippets of information concerning the Comanches from a number of dubious, not to say unsavoury, characters he had encountered along the way.

A small group of buffalo-hunters informed him that they had seen evidence of a number of large raiding-parties far to the north of the Comanches' normal range. Not long afterwards a dirty, greasy-looking young Mexican, whom he believed to be a Comanchero, disclosed that he had heard that a virulent cholera epidemic was sweeping through various Comanche bands. It struck Kane as being somewhat ironic that disease was the white man's most potent weapon in the fight against the savage tribes of the plains. The whole United States army had failed to achieve in twenty years what a few communicable diseases had managed in a quarter of the time.

Kane's information was well-received at the fort. A number of patrols were dispatched to intercept the war parties. In truth the troopers were only too happy to saddle up and ride away from the tedium of life on the post. Since the incident in Miller Springs the town had been put out of bounds to all ranks. It was a wise move given the bad blood that existed between the townsfolk and the regular soldiers.

A month after Kane's return to the post the ban

on visits to town had to be temporarily lifted. Lieutenant Ratcliffe was due in Miller Springs with his newly-wed bride. The scout was sent in with two veteran troopers to escort the officer and his wife back to the post.

Their arrival at the settlement was greeted with a mixture of open resentment, angry glances and whispered conversations. They were met by the new, recently-elected sheriff, Bob Bates. His welcome was perfunctory rather than cordial. 'I thought the army were staying out of my town?' he said firmly, before Kane was halfway out of the saddle.

'We're here to meet the noon stage,' replied the scout. 'One of the officers is due back from the east with his newly-wed wife. We're gonna see them back to the fort.'

A little of the tension drained from the peace-officer. 'I'd appreciate it if you and the troopers stayed out of the saloons.'

'Is that an order?' Bates thought he caught the merest fleeting hint of a smile on the scout's weather-beaten face. He liked Kane and was grateful for what he had done to set things right after the killings. However, his presence still made him feel uncomfortable. There were others in town, including Harmer's widow, who held the scout responsible for the popular storekeeper's death. He didn't want any further trouble.

'It's not an order, just a personal request,' he replied, choosing his words carefully.

'Fine,' said the scout, smiling mischievously. 'In that case we'll wait out here in the street until the stage arrives.' Bates touched his hat and strolled off back towards his office.

At a little after three the noon stage came into view as a distant speck of dust in the shimmering, hazy heat. Kane shielded his eyes from the glare of the sun and watched it draw steadily closer. The two troopers aboard the buckboard fidgeted uncomfortably in their itchy, hot tunics. Their discomfiture was due as much to the unfriendly stares of the various passers-by as the starchy material of their uniforms and the energy-sapping heat.

The stage pulled up in front of the depot in a great cloud of dust. 'What time yer got, Jake,' bawled the wizened old coot who was riding shotgun.

'It's a little after three,' replied the depot manager.

'Hell, Sam, we're early!' joked the driver, with a loud guffaw.

Ratcliffe and his lady were the last two passengers to disembark from the creaky, back-breaking, springless vehicle. The lieutenant grinned as soon as he caught sight of the scout. 'Hello, Kane,' he said, stepping forward to shake hands. 'To what do I owe this pleasure?'

'Just happened to be passing,' replied Kane, letting go of the lieutenant's hand.

Ratcliffe proceeded to introduce his lady. He then put their bags aboard the buckboard before helping Abigail into her seat. Only then did he notice the cold, unfriendly stares of the townsfolk. 'What's up with them?' he asked, motioning with his head towards the passing citizens.

Kane gave him a brief account of all that had happened. 'It's gonna take a long time for folks around here to forgive and forget,' advised Kane, when he had finished his account.

'I can imagine,' agreed Ratcliffe. 'It's a bad business.' With that he climbed into the buckboard alongside his love and the party began their long, hot journey back to Fort Walsh.

As the soldiers pulled out of town a dozen resentful faces turned to watch them leave. The looks on their faces said it all. They still looked upon the Yankee soldiers as an army of occupation. Memories of the war were still too vivid for most people to lay to rest. There had been many atrocities carried out during the conflict. Afterwards the carpet-baggers and tax-collectors had moved in under the protection of the cavalry to add to the Texans' suffering. All the resentment that had been simmering below the surface had erupted with a vengeance after the killings. There was bad blood between the town and the army. It would be a long time before it was forgotten.